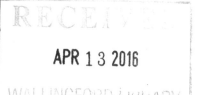

WING
&
CLAW

FOREST OF WONDERS

ALSO BY LINDA SUE PARK

NOVELS

Seesaw Girl

The Kite Fighters

A Single Shard

When My Name Was Keoko

Project Mulberry

Archer's Quest

Keeping Score

The 39 Clues: Storm Warning

A Long Walk to Water

The 39 Clues: Trust No One

PICTURE BOOKS

The Firekeeper's Son

Mung-Mung

What Does Bunny See?

Yum! Yuck!

Tap Dancing on the Roof

Bee-bim Bop!

The Third Gift

Xander's Panda Party

LINDA SUE PARK

WING
&
CLAW

FOREST OF WONDERS

ILLUSTRATED BY
JAMES MADSEN

HARPER
An Imprint of HarperCollinsPublishers

Library of Congress Control Number: 2015940700
ISBN 978-0-06-232738-3

Typography by Joe Merkel
Map by Mike Schley
16 17 18 19 20   CG/RRDH   10 9 8 7 6 5 4 3 2 1
❖
First Edition

To Kathleen, Vaunda, Vicky, Junko, Gail, Ken, Deb, Roxanne, Lisa, Louise, Sharon, Patty, Jeri, Elizabeth, and JoAnn, who know why

The Vast

Northern Slums

Shed
Compound

Stables

The Commons

Chancellery

Apothecary
Quarter

Garrison

Ferry
Landing

Forest of
Wonders

Everwide River

Farmsteads

The Mag

Raffa's
Home

Pother
Settlement

The Vast

PART I

CHAPTER ONE

RAFFA hesitated at the head of the steep stairs, a lantern in his hand. There was nothing wrong with going into the cellar, he told himself firmly.

His cousin, Garith, poked him from behind. "What are you waiting for?" he said. "We're not going to *do* anything. We're just having a look."

Easy for Garith to say—he wasn't the one who would be in the most trouble if they were caught! But Raffa's eagerness won out over his caution. He held the lantern higher, nerves tingling in anticipation.

The stairwell was lined with shelves holding earthenware jars, each carefully labeled. As he descended,

Raffa trailed his free hand along one row. A few jars were warm to the touch, and faint gleams of pale gold or green escaped from the edges of some of the cork stoppers. The wisps of scent in the air were intriguing—sweet, bitter, tantalizing, repulsive.

In the dark of the cellar, the lantern's glow illuminated more shelves. Chalked on one wall were the words FOR HEALING. These jars held dried and powdered botanicals to be made into poultices for rubbing on wounds and injuries. Another chalked sign read FOR CURING: jars containing plant essences for mixing into infusions and tonics to cure sickness. Raffa knew every one of them by heart.

"Where is it?" Garith asked, his voice too loud.

"Shussss," Raffa hissed. His parents and Uncle Ansel were in the garden, well out of earshot, but considering what the boys were about to do, Raffa thought it much wiser to be disobedient in whispers rather than shouts.

He swung the lantern toward the dark space under the stairs, where there was a small cabinet. In his father's careful lettering, a sign on its door read: FOR YEARNINGS.

Raffa had discovered the cabinet years earlier and had asked his parents about it several times. Mohan and Salima had always put aside these questions without answering, until finally, a few weeks ago, his father snapped at him, saying that it was no business for children.

Stung, Raffa had told Garith about the cabinet, and they had begun watching for a chance to investigate. Now, with the adults outside planning a new herb bed, the boys jostled shoulders under the stairs.

Garith had to crouch before the cabinet; a year older than Raffa, he was also more than a head taller. "There's nothing like this at our place," he said. "I mean, I'm allowed to use any botanical whenever I want."

Raffa did not reply. Unlike Garith, he was almost never allowed to work with botanicals unsupervised. They both knew this already, so why did Garith have to rub it in?

Holding his breath, Raffa pulled open the cabinet door. Six small jars . . . ordinary, humdrum. But a thrill rippled down his spine, for he knew that they might well hold apothecarial wonders.

Garith reached for one and uncorked it.

"You said we were only going to look!" Raffa protested. He glanced up at the stairs, as if his father might suddenly appear there.

"I *am* looking," Garith said as he peered into the jar. He sniffed at its contents, then grinned. "All right,

I lied—I'm smelling, too. Romarian, I think." Then his eyes lit up with mischief. "Let's make something!"

"Did you leave your brain at home?" Raffa exclaimed. "If my da finds out—"

"Look, it'll be easy," Garith cut in. "We'll take one of the jars and make a poultice. Even if they come in before we're done, we'll make sure there are other jars around as decoys, and we can put it back later. They'll never even know."

There was something about Garith that made it hard for people to say no to him, but beyond that, Raffa was more than a little tempted by the thought of doing apothecary work without Mohan watching over him. For the space of a single breath, he pitted the possibility of his father's wrath against the certainty of Garith's ridicule.

No contest.

"Just this once," Raffa said.

Back upstairs, the boys put several jars on the worktable. Each jar was labeled with the name of a single botanical, except for the one from the forbidden cabinet. In the bright daylight from the window, Raffa could now see the jar's three initials.

"C, R, D," he read aloud. He removed the stopper

and held the jar close to his nose. Green . . . piney . . . resiny. "You're right about the romarian. But I can't tell what else is in there."

"Califerium and dandelion," Garith guessed.

Raffa snorted. "Or coranthia and daynock. Or cressel and dill, or culpweed and dendra. What's the use of guessing?"

Garith shrugged. "You're the baby genius—you figure it out."

Raffa flushed. "Don't call me that!"

"Why not? Everyone else does."

"They do not."

"Maybe not to your face. But it's what they all think, and you know it. Besides, what's the problem? I wouldn't mind being called a genius."

It was the *baby* part that Raffa hated: He was all too aware of how much younger he looked than his twelve years. Round face, chubby cheeks. Big brown eyes and unruly curls. And he barely reached Garith's shoulder in height.

No one would ever call Garith a baby; he had grown so tall in the past year. Then again, it was true that no one would call him a genius, either.

Raffa poured small amounts of the powder into two

mortars and handed one to Garith. Each boy stirred in a little colza oil to form a paste. They were making a poultice to apply to the skin.

Apothecaries always tried out new treatments on their own skin first. Raffa knew this from his lessons, but he had never done it himself. His stomach quivered a little. So much more exciting than making the usual everyday poultices!

He turned the pestle rhythmically inside his mortar. The dull green paste thickened until it was almost like mud, then began belching big, slow bubbles. Raffa peered at the paste with interest; it wasn't the first time he'd seen a combination bubble, but it didn't happen often.

The more he stirred, the smaller the bubbles became and the faster they popped. Was this what the paste was supposed to do?

Then he heard a faint voice from outside; his head jerked up. Garith rushed to the window as Raffa snatched up the secret jar and looked around wildly for somewhere to hide it.

"It's okay—it was just my da laughing," Garith said. "They're still measuring. We're fine for a while yet."

The moment of panic had given Raffa an idea. Now

that the powder was in their mortars, they didn't need the jar any longer. So he returned it to its place in the cellar cabinet. Feeling a little more secure, he hurried up the stairs and focused his attention again on the paste in his mortar.

Something didn't seem quite right. The bubbles were still popping furiously, as if the paste were upset. In his mind, Raffa heard an unpleasant twang, and sensed somehow that the paste needed more liquid. The usual choices were water to dilute or oil to emulsify.

Then it came to him. Both. Oil *and* water.

His hand hovered for a moment between the oil cruet and the water jar, as if giving himself a last chance to choose one or the other. He banished his doubts and added a few more drops of oil plus a tiny spoonful of water.

The paste grew smooth and silken. The twanging sound faded away.

For as long as Raffa could remember, he had possessed a keen instinct for apothecary. At times, combining botanicals felt to him like mixing colors, adding ingredients until the hues in his mind matched or complemented each other. But he didn't like to use the word *visions*, as some in the settlement did when speaking of him. It made him sound like a wobbler.

Besides, it wasn't always colors. Sometimes, like now, it was sounds. Or shapes, or light and darkness. He never knew quite how it would come to him, but the results were invariable: His botanical concoctions were pure and strong, clear or gleaming, as fine as those produced by apothecaries with decades of practice.

Raffa's instinctive abilities puzzled both his parents; his father, especially, seemed more troubled than pleased. Talent, Mohan said, was no substitute for experience, and he repeatedly cautioned Raffa about the danger of relying on instinct. But the intuitions had grown stronger over the years, and as hard as he tried to heed his father, Raffa found them impossible to ignore.

"Mine's ready," Garith declared.

Raffa took a furtive peek at Garith's paste. It looked ill-stirred, with a rough, grainy texture. He sighed inwardly. Garith hated it when his pastes and tinctures didn't turn out as well as Raffa's, but he didn't like to be corrected, either.

"Good," Raffa said, a fingertip poised above his mortar. "We should hurry—they might come in soon. On the backs of our hands first, okay?"

"Boring," Garith replied immediately. "Uncle Mohan

wouldn't have stored this combination unless he'd already tested it, right? Let's try it on our faces. And the sign says 'For Yearnings,' so we should yearn for something."

Raffa shook his head doubtfully. Since his first glimpse of the cabinet, he had wondered about the word *yearnings*. It was a curious word for an apothecary to use. Contrary to what many city folk thought, apothecaries were not magicians with the ability to grant wishes.

"Do you really think that's what it means?" he asked.

"I don't know, but what could it hurt?" Garith replied.

"Fine," Raffa said. "What should we yearn for?"

After a quick discussion, it was decided that Raffa would yearn for less chubby cheeks, while Garith would yearn for the disappearance of the small mole above his right jawline.

"Together," Raffa said. Tense with both curiosity and anticipation, he rubbed some of the paste on his cheekbones as Garith did the same to his jaw.

Nothing happened. No tingling or warmth or tightening. No stinging. No itch.

"Huh," Garith said after a few moments. "Maybe *yearnings* means combinations Uncle Mohan wishes would work when, really, they're total duds."

Raffa knew his father better than that: Mohan would not have kept and hidden a useless combination. Why wasn't it doing anything?

"Well, that was a garble," Garith said in disgust.

They cleaned up the work area quickly, and a few moments later, when the adults came in, they found the boys sitting at the table studying apothecarial charts.

"Earnestness and virtue!" Garith's father, Ansel, exclaimed as he entered the cabin, followed by Raffa's parents. He patted Raffa on the back heartily.

Raffa's mother, Salima, raised her eyebrows. "Yes, studying without being ordered to," she said. "A welcome and wholly unexpected sign of maturity."

Everyone laughed—except Mohan. He looked first at Raffa, then at Garith, and back at Raffa again. In a quiet, cold voice, he asked, "What the shakes have you been doing?"

Raffa felt his insides shrivel. He cast a quick look at Garith—and his heart missed a beat.

Garith's jaw on one side had suddenly swollen into a fist-sized lump that pulsed and quivered like a bullfrog's throat. The lump was etched with blue veins. Raffa stared wide-eyed as Garith reached up to touch his jaw and uttered a gargled cry.

The lump rippled and trembled as if it were made of jelly. It looked so odd that Raffa almost had to choke back a laugh. Then realization hit him: *If Garith's jaw is swollen, what does my own face look like?*

With a shiver of dread, he raised his hands to his cheeks. They felt . . . completely normal!

But just as he began to exhale in relief, Salima's hand flew to her mouth. "Raffa!"

"Quake's sake!" Uncle Ansel exclaimed.

Raffa jumped to his feet and hurried to the mirror on the shelf near the door. Holding his breath, he forced himself to look in the glass—and cried out.

CHAPTER TWO

THE blood vessels in his cheeks were glowing bright blue!

Raffa rubbed frantically at the blue veins, which made them glow even brighter. Salima led him back to the table, put a hand under his chin, and tilted his head to examine him more closely.

"Stop rubbing," she said. "No pain? Or warmth? And for you, Garith?"

Both boys shook their heads.

"I judge that your lives are not in danger," Salima said. "Raffa, whatever were you thinking?"

"The cabinet under the stairs," Mohan said grimly.

He turned to Ansel. "I keep a few combinations that Raffa is not allowed to work with. It seems that these two have gotten into them. What they did not realize is that I have not finished testing them—as the boys have plainly proved."

Raffa didn't need to see his father's glare; he could feel it like heat all around him.

"Ah," Ansel said. "What are these combinations intended for?"

A brief silence. It was Salima who answered. "Mohan plans to work with them further to see if they might help with certain yearnings."

"Yearnings!" Ansel exclaimed. "Well, that *is* a surprise. What exactly—"

"A conversation for another time," Mohan cut in. "For the moment, we have two garblers to deal with."

Garblers were careless apothecaries, or poorly trained ones. Or worst of all, those who knowingly made false claims of miracle cures. Such shammers brought the very art of apothecary into disrepute. Raffa's face reddened. He was no garbler! It was utterly unfair of his father to call him one.

"A veraloe and willow-bark combination should take care of that," Mohan said, indicating Garith's jaw. "But it seems that Raffa used something different?"

Raffa was too humiliated to speak.

"It was the same jar," Garith muttered. "He just added more oil and a little water."

Now it was Ansel who looked angry. "Will you never learn?" he said to Garith. "You are swollen; Raffa is not. It is precisely those kinds of small details that make a difference!"

Salima addressed Mohan and Ansel. "I suggest that an appropriate punishment would be to cancel this afternoon's outing."

Both boys groaned. They had been promised a trip to the market—the big one that took place only once every two months.

"Agreed," Ansel said. "I do not approve of the disobedience. But it seems to me that the curiosity and eagerness behind the disobedience ought to be . . . perhaps not applauded but at least addressed, wouldn't you say?"

"To be precise about this," Mohan said, "it was Raffa who disobeyed, even though Garith should have known better. Raffa, you will spend the next three mornings mucking the vegetable beds."

Raffa froze his expression. He would not give his father the satisfaction of a reaction.

An uncomfortable silence. Ansel shrugged. "We had better be going." With a quick wink at Raffa, he took Garith by the arm and departed.

As Raffa sat, his head bowed glumly, Salima set about making an antidote paste. Neither she nor Mohan had ever seen anything quite like Raffa's glowing veins, so she combined hazeltine and wortjon, the usual treatment for venous complaints.

As she applied the paste to Raffa's cheeks, she said, "So then. Yearnings."

Mohan grumbled something inaudible.

"No, husband. Ansel is right. Raffa's disobedience is a clear sign that we can no longer ignore his curiosity. Far better for him to learn the truth from us than falsehoods from others."

Another grumble from Mohan, but he said nothing more. Raffa leaned forward eagerly. At last he was to learn how apothecary could possibly have anything to do with yearnings.

"Some people . . . Let's see, how can I put it nicely? Some people are not fully aware of the true nature of our work," Salima said. "They seek botanica to satisfy their hearts' desires. Great wealth, love, power—things no infusion or paste can produce. But the truth might as well not exist to those who refuse to believe it."

"There are even some who suspect us of keeping such potions to ourselves out of selfishness," Mohan said, his voice a low growl. "The stupidity! What are they thinking—that we have made ourselves fabulously wealthy but are hiding all evidence of it?"

Salima went on, "People's yearnings are as varied as their imaginations. I remember a young poet"— she rolled her eyes—"demanding a paste that could be applied to the hand, to produce better poems!"

"Over the years, we turned them all away," said Mohan, who seemed a good deal calmer now. "They finally learned to take their idiocies elsewhere—to garblers."

"I understand about silly requests like that," Raffa said. "But then, why the cabinet?"

Mohan was silent for a moment. "It's complicated," he said at last. "Perhaps when you're older."

Raffa put his hands under the table so he could clench his fists out of Mohan's sight. When would his father stop treating him like a baby? He swallowed his anger. "How do you know if something is a yearning?" he asked.

"To fly like a bird? To become wealthy in an instant?

Surely it's clear that no concoction could have such powers!" Mohan's brow tightened with displeasure.

"Yes, of course," Raffa said hastily. "But what about
things like—" He searched his mind for a good example.
"Like sleeping infusions?"

"What about them?"

Raffa spoke slowly in an effort to sound grown-up
and thoughtful. "People who don't sleep well—their
lives are miserable because they're always tired, right?
And then someone discovers combinations to help people sleep better. But before that, if someone had said, 'I
wish I could sleep well just one night in my life,' would
that have been a yearning?"

Mohan looked surprised. Salima clapped her hands.
"Well done, Raffa!" she said. "Your question is a good
one. Someday, your father and I would like to study ailments that cannot yet be cured. The yearnings for such
cures are deep and desperate. But if a desire has nothing
to do with health, then it is a foolish yearning."

Raffa nodded once, then reversed himself and shook
his head. "Couldn't something *seem* foolish at first, but
then, after we experiment and try things and learn more,
it turns out not to be foolish after all?"

"That is precisely the point!" Mohan said. "These

things take much time and thought. You cannot rush in and experiment like a reckless wobbler. No good comes of it!" He glared pointedly at Raffa's cheeks.

Raffa lowered his head. Why couldn't Da have told him about the yearnings cabinet long before this? He had never known that his parents were even vaguely interested in experimentation: His father's sole pursuit had always been the treatment of patients, with the usual combinations. Why wasn't he excited about discovering what apothecary could do to help people even more?

Raffa seethed. As long as he was under Mohan's watchful eye, he would never be able to make those kinds of discoveries, either.

Mohan and Salima left for the market. Raffa went out to the dooryard. It was a clear autumn day, both breezy and sunny. A perfect day for an outing, he thought with a sigh.

Raffa sat on a bench under the eaves and began to carve wooden stoppers for his jars, smaller versions of those kept in the cellar. He wanted his own stock of botanica, separate from that of his parents.

Cork dust and crumbs fell at his feet. As he was finishing the last of the stoppers, he heard a noise overhead.

It sounded like a kitten mewling. Raffa looked up, puzzled, just in time to see a small dark blob fall out of the sky straight toward him.

He ducked and covered his head with his hands. Something hit his elbow, and he flung out his arm to cast it away. A moment later he heard a sickening thud when whatever it was hit the partly opened wooden shutter and dropped into the cabin.

Raffa leapt to his feet and peered into the window. But it was too dark; he saw nothing but shadows on the floor. The mewling had stopped.

He hurried to the door and stepped inside. There it was, on the floor beneath the window, a dark heap no bigger than the palm of his hand.

Raffa approached slowly. He saw a little movement and heard a single mewl, much weaker and fainter this time.

"A bat," he whispered.

About the size of a field mouse with wings, the little bat was badly injured. Its wings were torn in several places, the left one barely more than ribbons and tatters. Raffa guessed that it had been attacked by a bird of prey. His guess proved correct when he discovered an owl feather clutched in one of the bat's tiny talons.

The right wing had at least two broken bones in

it—which could have happened, Raffa realized, when he flung the bat away. He immediately felt guilty about having added to the creature's suffering. The poor thing had to be in terrible pain.

Could he treat the bat for its injuries? On his own? He had been preparing combinations as well as making poultices and infusions for years now, but always with one of his parents—usually Mohan—at his side, watching and commenting on what seemed like his every move. Most of what Raffa was allowed to do was simple and repetitive, standard combinations for common ailments that were bothersome but hardly life-threatening.

The bat seemed almost like a gift: a chance to work on serious injuries by himself, and to prove that he wasn't a garbler! But what if he failed? Or made things worse?

The bat let out another sound—a weak but agonized squeal. The pitiful sound decided things for Raffa: He might fail, but he had to try.

Select the right botanica. Prepare the paste. Apply it to the bat's injuries. Bind every one of the many rips and tears. Splint the tiny wing bones.

For splints, Raffa used matchsticks, the smallest and straightest pieces of wood he could find. Then he carefully moved the bat, which he now knew was a male, into a box lined with milkweed fluff. Finally he draped the box with one of his mother's woolen shawls.

Raffa lost all track of time. He only realized that he had spent most of the afternoon treating the bat when his neck and shoulders cramped up from being bent over the tiny creature for so long.

As he straightened and rolled his shoulders, he heard hoofbeats, followed moments later by his mother's voice.

"Raffa? We're back!"

Mohan and Salima came in carrying sacks heavy with market goods. "Oh, good," Salima said. "That strange boy with the blue-veined cheeks is gone, and our Raffa is back again. We missed you, darling!" She ruffled his hair, and Raffa knew that she, at least, had forgiven him.

In his preoccupation with the bat, Raffa had forgotten all about his cheeks. He realized how lucky he had been that the effects of the poultice were so short-lived, and he hoped that Garith's jaw was back to normal as well.

"What's this?" Mohan asked, nodding at the box.

"A bat," Raffa said. "It's wounded. Badly."

"In that case, thank goodness you used my best shawl," Salima said drily.

Mohan strode across the room. "You've already

treated it? By yourself?" He lifted the shawl and inspected the bat.

I don't see anyone else here, do you? Raffa wanted to say. He drew in a breath to stop those words and chose others instead. "I used the combination for slashes," he said. "But I added some arnicullus."

"Why arnicullus?" Mohan's face was expressionless.

"Because, um—" Raffa searched for a way to answer without telling the whole truth: that he had seen the wrong colors in his mind. His intuition had told him that the poultice needed something more.

"I'm pretty sure it was attacked by an owl," he said. "That's not the same as being slashed by a blade. So I—I thought to add another healing botanical."

He saw his parents exchange glances.

"I don't suppose you knew," Mohan said slowly, "that arnicullus is combined with burdock and zinjal to treat a rare sickness transmitted by birds?"

Raffa shook his head.

"Hmph," Mohan said. "Well. We'll have to wait and see."

Raffa took the bat's box to a warm corner near the stove. As he began to help put away the market goods, he kept his excitement to himself. His first real experiment!

Well, his second, really, if he counted the garble with the jar from the cabinet.

Would it be a success? Da was right about one thing, anyway: He'd have to wait and see.

CHAPTER THREE

THE next morning, Raffa opened his eyes in the earliest light of daybirth. He crept to the end of the pallet and peered into the box.

It was too dark to see clearly. He heard no sound, nor did he detect any movement, and yet . . . the bat was still alive. He didn't know how he knew—just a feeling that the stillness in the box was not the stillness of death.

Carefully he carried the box to the window ledge and opened the shutters. A swash of sunlight fell over the little mound in the box, and Raffa saw movement under the corner of the linen rag that his mother had given him after rescuing her shawl.

He lifted the rag and saw that the bat was indeed still breathing. The matchstick splints had held during the night, and Raffa felt confident that the wee bones would knit and mend.

But a cautious peek under one of the bindings revealed the other wing to be a fearsome sight, the webbing a ragged mess. If the bat lived, its wing would be useless. What good would survival be to a bat that couldn't fly?

Raffa listened to the bat's labored breathing a few moments longer. Then he went out to the garden to find his father. Mohan always rose before dawn to begin his work; some plants were best harvested while still pearled with night-dew.

He found his father in the califer bed, harvesting the seedpods used to make califerium, one of the most useful of botanica. Depending on what it was combined with, califerium could soothe tremors, calm anxiety, or induce sleep, but by far its most important property was its ability to ease pain.

In the wrong hands, it could also be extremely dangerous. On its own, a dose of pure essence of califerium could be fatal. It required other botanicals to balance its deadly effects.

Raffa had a particular pride concerning califerium.

Local lore had it that the califer plant was unknown in the region until the Santana family—his own ancestors—brought seeds of the plant with them from the far southwest, when they migrated to Obsidia more than two hundred years before he was born.

"Da?" Raffa called out as he approached.

Mohan's hands did not stop moving, but he nodded by way of greeting. "Did the little thing make it through?"

So Mohan had not checked on the bat himself. Raffa was glad that his father wasn't interfering, but to his surprise he also felt a shudder of doubt. The bat was so badly hurt, it would need the best of care to survive, and didn't that mean someone older, wiser, more experienced than himself?

He nodded. "But his wing still looks really terrible, Da," he said. "The paste I made was good, I think, but he needs something even better."

"It was very badly injured," Mohan said gruffly. "You know well that there are times when our art, even at its best, is not enough."

Raffa put one hand in the pocket of his tunic, as if he were keeping his courage there. "Da," he said, "I want to go to the Forest. To see if I can find something that might help."

Mohan shook his head. "Your mother went only three days ago. She would not go again so soon. And I cannot spare the time."

Raffa had expected this response; he had never been allowed to go to the Forest of Wonders by himself. Salima went there to gather wild plants at least twice monthly. Uncle Ansel was among the few who ventured into its deepest heart, where there were no paths, little light, and much that was unknown. But Mohan hardly ever visited the Forest, preferring to work with garden botanicals.

It wasn't that the Forest was a perilous place so much as it was utterly unpredictable. The main danger was losing one's way: Raffa had heard of people who had entered the Forest and never been seen again. New and mysterious plants appeared at capricious intervals; a familiar path might look completely different from week to week. Large beasts of prey were rare, but there had been sightings of bear and wolf. Those who would visit had to observe keenly, step lightly, and keep a steady compass in their heads. And Raffa knew that his father did not believe him capable of all that.

He tightened the fist inside his pocket. "I was wondering," he said, "if I might go on my own."

Mohan had begun shaking his head even before Raffa finished his sentence. "How will you find your way? You might wander into the interior and lose yourself there. No, you will have to wait until your mother's next trip."

"But, Da, it will be too late!" Raffa rushed on before his father could say anything more. "He's fighting so hard to live, and—and if there's something in the Forest that might help, I want to try to find it. And I'll be really careful and stay on the paths and only go to the places I know, and I'll be home way before it gets dark."

"Home from where?"

Salima had come out of the henhouse and was walking toward them. Raffa knew that his only chance was to get her on his side.

"I want to go to the Forest, Mam. To try to find something that might help the bat."

"And what does your father have to say about it?"

For answer, Raffa stared at the ground.

"We could do it by stages," Salima suggested. "The next time I go, Raffa, you could take the lead and I'll follow. Perhaps even out of earshot. What would you say to that?"

Raffa clenched his jaw to make sure that he spoke his next words carefully. "It's a good idea, Mam. But I have to go *today*. I know it's only a bat, but you've seen how sick he is and—and I'm the one who's been treating him, so he's my responsibility. If I can't find something to help him soon . . ."

They stood in a triangle of awkward silence. As the silence lengthened, Raffa's despair grew to match it.

At last Mohan plucked one final pod and threw it into the barrow. "There is a vine," he said.

Raffa frowned, a moment of confusion followed by bitter disappointment at the change of subject. Yet more evidence of how his father saw him—as a child whose requests didn't matter.

Mohan went on, "It has great powers of healing. Years ago, my grandmother found it, and used it to save a badly burned child. It seemed to have potent abilities to heal injured flesh. She had only a small supply, and she never found the vine again. Your mother and I look for it every time we go to the Forest, but we've never been able to find it, either. We think it may be a plant that leafs out only rarely."

Why was Da telling him this?

"You have done fine work with the bat, Raffa," Mohan said quietly. "And you have convinced me that your request is made in the spirit of a true apothecary."

"Agreed," Salima said, with a nod and a smile.

Raffa felt a pinprick of hope. Was it possible—could they be considering—

"You may go to the Forest to search for the vine on one condition," Mohan said, raising a cautionary hand. "You cannot go alone. Garith must go with you."

"Oh, lovely idea," Salima said. "They may as well sail the Vast together while they're at it. What are you thinking—that at least they'll have each other's company while they lose their way?"

"Garith is a year older," Mohan pointed out.

"Yes, but not a year wiser," Salima responded.

Raffa would have smiled if he weren't so anxious to hear her decision.

"But I think you may be right," Salima said, after a pause. "Between the two of them, they ought to be able to string together enough sensible moments to get there and back in one piece."

Raffa's mouth fell open. He felt like whooping and capering right there in the califerium patch. Going with Garith was the perfect compromise.

"Where did your grandmother find it?" he asked eagerly.

"Perhaps a half morning in," Mohan said, lifting

his chin toward the north, where the Forest lay. "The stem and leaves are scarlet, axils pale green. Small fleshy leaves that grow in profusion close to the stem, and I seem to recall that they were opposing, not alternating."

"If we find it, we'll bring back as much as we can carry," Raffa said.

Mohan nodded. "Be home well before nightfall. Banish all rashness. And do not leave the paths." A pause. "You have the mucking to do, but you may begin tomorrow."

Raffa had already turned to go. "Mam, Da, thank you!" he called over his shoulder as he raced back to the cabin, his feet barely touching the ground.

With a picnic lunch in his rucksack, Raffa hurried to his cousin's cabin on the other side of the pother settlement. Both he and Garith knew the path between their homes so well that they could walk it sure-footed even on moonless nights. The boys had apothecary lessons with Mohan together, and it was rare for them to spend longer than a day or two without each other's company.

Garith, whose jawline was back to normal, readily agreed to the outing. He had never been to the Forest on his own, either, but not for the same reason as Raffa. Uncle Ansel would have allowed him to go by himself anytime, but Garith was too social a creature to want to make such a trip alone.

The boys started off on the lane that cut through the heart of the pother settlement. To Raffa's surprise, there was a sizeable gathering in the square, even though it wasn't a market day.

On the steps of the meetinghouse, which served as an informal outdoor stage, two men were waiting for the crowd to assemble. By their fine clothes, Raffa could tell that they were city dwellers, probably from Gilden, the capital, which was a good half day away by wagon and ferry.

"What are they about?" Raffa asked Garith, who shrugged.

"Dunno. Maybe we should go back and tell my da."

But there was no need, for they turned to see Ansel on the path behind them, already on his way to join the crowd. He waved at them, then stopped to speak to someone in the square.

"Should we stay and find out what's going on?" Garith asked.

Raffa considered for a moment, then shook his head. "I promised Da I'd be home well before dark, and it might take us a long time to find the vine."

As they continued through the settlement, they saw people they knew, some of them apothecaries or their children, others who were patients. To Raffa's great annoyance, Mannum Zimmer, the cobbler, greeted him by chucking him under the chin, then held up his hand to match palms with Garith.

"Off adventuring, boys?" he said.

"Yes," Raffa replied as he took a step away from Garith, hoping to make the difference in their height less noticeable. "To the Forest."

Mannum Zimmer made an expression of mock horror. "Visit the Forest, come out the sorest," he said, repeating a silly saying used by city folk.

Rarely did anyone other than the apothecaries visit the Forest of Wonders; there were other wooded areas for hunting and timber. Those from Gilden spoke in awed whispers of the Forest's arcane magic. Plants with tendrils that could strangle . . . shrubs that shot out poisonous thorns . . . flowers whose scents induced eternal sleep. Who could even imagine the beasts that fed on such dreadful flora? And what of the gnomers and throlls and other fantastic creatures from once upon a time—weren't there always kernels of truth in such stories?

Only kernels. There was, for instance, the touchrue

bush, whose thorns were not only needle-sharp but also coated with a sap that burned painfully. The bush did not, however, launch its thorns. But it suited the pothers to keep the Forest both pristine and to themselves, so in general they said as little as possible to refute the rumors.

"Don't worry, Mannum Zimmer. We'll be careful," Garith said cheerfully.

Other friends stopped the boys to inquire about their families. Mohan Santana and Salima Vale were more than well-respected for their apothecarial abilities, while Salima's brother, Ansel, was admired for his boldness and adventurous spirit. Garith, with his easy manner, was a great favorite with young and old alike. As for Raffa—he knew too well what was said about him in the settlement.

Baby genius, indeed.

He was in no mood to hear that again, besides which he was in a hurry to get to the Forest. "Come on," he said to Garith. "We can pretend we're foot-racing. Then it won't seem rude to people when we run past them."

"RumbletumbleGO!" Garith shouted, without warning. He took off, leaving Raffa flat-footed behind him.

"Hey!" Raffa charged after his cousin.

It took a good few minutes for Raffa to catch up,

and he managed it only because Garith slowed to a walk once he was beyond the settlement.

"Thought you'd never get here," Garith said lazily as Raffa came puffing up beside him.

"Maybe someday you won't need such a big head start to beat me," Raffa shot back.

They continued their friendly bickering as the Mag came into view. The Mag was a bleak wasteland that covered a long stretch bordering the Forest. It was named for the magma that had risen to the surface when a deep fissure opened up during the Quake.

The Great Quake. Some two hundred years earlier, a series of violent earth tremors had devastated half the continent. Millions had died; whole cities had been destroyed. The destruction was on a scale never before experienced in recorded history. The Sudden Mountains were born, a range of peaks and abysses that all but isolated Obsidia from neighboring lands to the south and west.

In the aftermath of the Quake, small groups of people had made the perilous journey to Gilden and its environs, which were the only sites within hundreds of miles to escape total devastation. Raffa's Santana ancestors had made the arduous trek from the southwest to cross the Suddens, and for every family that reached its destination, many more had died trying.

Although not nearly as imposing as the mountains, the Mag was still an effective barrier between the settlement and the Forest. Even in full daylight, it was an eerie place. Twisted rock formations rose from the pitted basalt underfoot, some of them three times Raffa's height. Others littered the ground like small creatures from another world, frozen in midstep. Some of the more distinctive formations had names: the Angry Ox, the Frozen Man, the Poisoned Pillar.

Well before sunpeak, the boys passed the Three-Headed Beaster, which was the last significant Mag formation before the Forest. Tree growth began with young saplings pushing their way through the tall grass along the path. It was a pleasant part of the walk, a few moments of relief between the harshness of the Mag and the strangeness of the Forest. Raffa was torn between delight and anxiety: What surprises would the Forest have in store today?

"Whew," Garith said, and stopped to drink from his waterskin. He peered ahead down the steadily narrowing path. "It would be nicer to eat here, don't you think? Rather than farther in, where it'll be a lot darker."

"We haven't even started looking yet," Raffa said,

anxious to reach the Forest proper.

"But if we eat now, our packs will be lighter," Garith pointed out. "And we'll have more room to carry stuff if we find anything."

Raffa rolled his eyes. No one could keep Garith and food apart for very long. If they didn't stop to eat now, Raffa knew that his cousin would badger him mercilessly. Besides, he was a little hungry, too. So he shrugged out of his rucksack's straps while Garith found them a handy stump to sit on not far off the path.

Raffa's rucksack contained flaky oatcakes spread with good butter, two small chunks of crumbly cheese, slices of onion, and a handful of dried cherries.

"Solid-earth, look what else!" Garith exclaimed in delight. As a surprise treat, Salima had given them pieces of honeycomb wrapped in grapevine leaves.

The boys settled down to contented chewing. A few curious chickadees flitted around, calling, "Chicka-dee-dee-dee!" Raffa threw crumbs to the little birds. He liked them for their friendliness and their neat black caps and bibs.

In the midst of lunch, Garith started a cherry pit–spitting contest. He won the first few rounds easily. Then Raffa argued that because Garith was taller, he should have to stand back a step for the next round.

"That's the only way we can see who's *really* spitting them farther," Raffa concluded.

"You're just mad because I beat you three times in a row," Garith said.

"So? If you're so sure you're better at it, you shouldn't be worried about taking a step back."

After some more discussion, Garith agreed to take *half* a step back. The spit that followed was a tie—at least the way Raffa saw it.

"No, mine won," Garith declared. "Yours landed on a leaf—it's higher than mine, not farther."

"That's horsedawdle and you know it!"

"Is not!"

"Is so!"

Garith let out a pretend roar and tackled his cousin. They rolled around in the underbrush until the rassle ended with both boys breathless and laughing.

Raffa sat up and brushed dead leaves from his hair. Then he plucked a small twig out of his tunic and his mood suddenly turned somber: The twig reminded him of the matchsticks he had used to splint the bat's wing.

He jumped to his feet. "Come on," he said. "We need to get going."

CHAPTER FOUR

THE boys walked single file now, rather than side by side. Garith led the way. Since they had reached the interior, the trees were taller and closer together, straining the sun's rays and dimming their light. Phosphorescent fungi glowed in mossy shadows. It was a place of whispers and secrets.

The path was almost, but not quite, the same as it had been on Raffa's last visit. There was a dense grove of bamboo-like trees he didn't remember, and parts of the trail were now edged with scratchy spikes of orange beardgrass, which he'd only seen previously in another part of the Forest.

Otherwise, he recognized the way easily, to his relief. If the area had changed too much, he might have wished that his mother were with him, which was not the kind of doubt he wanted to feel on this trip.

His pace slowed as he peered around intently, searching for a flash of red amid all the greenery. Meanwhile, Garith was supposedly looking for the vine, too. But there were plenty of fine distractions around. The Forest of Wonders was mostly old growth; some of its trees had been alive for centuries, even surviving the Great Quake. It held countless smaller wonders, too.

"Raffa—cracklefruit! I've never seen them so late in the year!" Garith bounded a few yards off the path to a small shrub. He returned with a handful of the pale yellow orbs and gave two to Raffa. The cousins watched each other's mouth to see the bright sparks flash from the fruits as they were crunched.

Next Garith found a stand of burstbean stalks. He collected several pods and spent the next few minutes throwing them at tree trunks. Each pod exploded with a loud bang that clearly annoyed the trees' residents— squirrels and jays, who chattered and scolded noisily.

Raffa picked some pods, too, and put them into his rucksack. As far as he knew, no one had yet found an apothecarial use for them, but that didn't mean there wasn't one. He could experiment, try new combinations. . . .

Then something else caught his eye. "Look at this," he said, stepping up to a neverbare tree that flanked the path. The bark bore several long, deep scratches caked with hardened resin. Caught in the resin was a tuft of coarse blond fur.

"Bear," he said in awe. Bears were a rarity in the Forest. Not even Uncle Ansel had ever seen one, although he sometimes reported having seen signs of them deep in the interior.

"Do you think it's the one—you know, tamed by that girl?" Garith asked.

Some settlement folk claimed that a girl from one of the nearby farmsteads had tamed a Forest bear. Neither Raffa nor Garith had ever met her.

"How would I know?" Raffa said, fingering the fur. He tried to imagine what it might be like to tame a bear. Was it like training a dog? Did you start with *sit* and *stay*? Could a wild bear ever become as tame as a pet?

These thoughts brought his mind back to the little bat again, and he chided himself for idling. He knew he would not have been allowed this trip if Mohan had thought that other botanicals might keep the bat alive.

The scarlet vine was the bat's only chance.

Raffa put his head down and began the search again in earnest. With his eyes on the forest floor, he didn't see Garith come to a halt, and bumped into him. "What—" he started to ask.

"Wait." Garith held up his hand. "It's weird," he said, his brow furrowed in puzzlement. "There's some kind of clearing up ahead. A big one. See how light it is?"

Raffa leaned around his cousin to get a better look. Garith was right. The path continued on through dense growth, but by looking up instead of down, Raffa could see that it was much brighter ahead of them.

He tried to think. When was the last time he had been in this part of the Forest? Last spring, probably— maybe six months ago. There hadn't been any clearing back then.

The boys moved forward cautiously. Then Raffa let out a sound that was half cry, half groan as he stared at the scene before them.

Dozens of trees had been ruthlessly axed, their doomed trunks forming a haphazard border around the clearing. There was no way to replace such venerable trees, not in his lifetime, not in his children's children's lifetimes. This was no Forest magic. It was human-wrought.

The clearing had obviously been some kind of camp, abandoned only recently. Off-center, a ring of stones and a pile of blackened wood showed where a fire had been.

The boys walked the perimeter of the clearing in silence. Piles of rubbish littered the ground. Raffa saw a forgotten tent stake. A torn waterskin. Pieces of frayed rope. Whoever the intruders were, they had been careless and slovenly.

Approaching the far side of the clearing, they could see that a track had been hacked through the Forest, heading northwest and wide enough for a cart or even a small wagon. A chill trickled down Raffa's spine. There were trails throughout the Forest, but no roads or tracks. It was part of the charter.

The Forest had been protected by government charter for centuries because of its essential botanica, without which countless ailments could not be healed or cured. "For use by all, abuse by none" was the motto in the charter. Whoever slashed this track through the Forest had broken the law as well as ruined the land. There might be an explanation for everything here, but Raffa couldn't think of one.

Who would do such a thing? And why?

"I think we should follow the track," Garith said at

last. "If we can figure out where it goes, maybe we'll get an idea of who did this."

Raffa shuffled his feet. "Do you think—I mean, maybe we should—"

"Should what?"

"I don't know. . . . Tell someone first?"

"What, are you scared?"

Raffa stifled a sigh. He wasn't scared. There was a difference between scared and cautious, but he'd never be able to explain that to Garith.

So they made their way to the track. As they took their first steps out of the clearing, there was a *whoosh* in the air above their heads, and an enormous bird hurtled past, barely missing them.

"Hey!" Garith shouted. "What was *that*?"

Raffa turned to watch the bird as it soared behind them. It was a great-tufted owl, easily the biggest he had ever seen. It banked in a smooth curve, barely moving a feather—then headed back toward them.

"Look out!" he yelled and ducked.

The owl came at them again, its vicious talons extended for a strike. The boys stopped short and reversed direction.

Again and again, the owl circled and dove at them.

Raffa could see its yellow eyes fierce with concentration.

What was going on? Owls didn't attack people—and what was this one doing out in the middle of the day, anyway?

They fled through the clearing and back to the path. "Where is it?" Garith panted, his eyes wide as he turned in a full circle, looking for the deranged bird.

A tense silence, during which the boys could hear nothing but their own ragged breathing.

Then—

Wham!

"*Yow!*" Garith yelled. He dove to one side of the path, Raffa right beside him. Both boys covered their heads with their hands and cowered there, motionless.

After a few moments, Raffa dared a peek, then sat up and looked around. There was no sign of the owl.

Garith was clutching the top of his head. Blood trickled slowly down his forehead.

"Garith! You're hurt!"

"I'm okay," Garith said in a shaky voice. "Just a scratch."

Quickly Raffa untied the kerchief knotted to his rucksack, took out his waterskin, and dampened the cloth. He would have stanched the wound himself, but Garith waved him off and took the kerchief from him.

Raffa scrambled around on his hands and knees in the undergrowth. Mellia or wortjon didn't grow this deep in the Forest, but he found a few wilted yellow-root leaves. What could he combine them with? There had to be something. . . . He scanned the plant life around him.

There! Growing on the north side of a huge querco tree was a large colony of sponge moss. Raffa dug out a small patch with his penknife. As he rubbed the moss and leaves together between his palms, he saw blue and red blending to pale lavender in his head. It should have been a deep rich violet, but without mortar and pestle, the paste was very crude.

It would have to do. He patted the paste on the wound, doing the best he could to rub it through Garith's hair and into his scalp. All the while, he puzzled over the behavior of the crazed owl.

Then he remembered that the bat had been clutching an owl feather: It, too, had been attacked by an owl. Could it have been the same bird?

"I'm all right," Garith repeated. "Thanks—it's already stopped bleeding. Let's just sit here and rest a minute."

Raffa sat down with his back against the querco tree. His heart was still pounding, and he closed his eyes for a few moments. A breeze riffled the leaves, but otherwise the Forest was quiet.

The tree at his back was ancient and enormous. If both boys had stood with their arms outstretched, they might just have been able to encircle the trunk. Raffa opened his eyes, thinking of how the roots reached as deep into the earth as the topmost twigs stretched into the sky. The entire root system would be equal in girth to the tree's crown, as if two huge trees had been placed as mirror images above and below the ground.

As he stared into the branches of the tree, his vision seemed to cloud. One of the branches became a shelf, like those in the cellar back home, holding a single earthenware jar. He took a breath, and the image vanished.

He squinted in puzzlement. Near the trunk, a bright red snake twined itself around the limb. That was a little unusual; most of the snakes in the Forest were more modest colors, gray or black or brown. Out near the end of the branch where it forked, there was a large ball of leaves and twigs, a squirrel's drey, but it looked abandoned—

Raffa blinked. He flicked his gaze back along the branch.

A bright red snake?

CHAPTER FIVE

RAFFA jumped to his feet and pointed. "Garith! Do you see it? That streak of red?"

It wasn't a snake at all.

It was a vine!

That was why the branch had turned into a shelf in his mind's eye! He must have seen the vine without realizing it, and only now recognized it for what it was.

Garith stayed seated, still holding the kerchief to his head. He looked up into the tree.

"You think that could be it?" he asked, sounding dubious.

"No wonder they couldn't find it—it grows in the

trees, not on the ground!" Raffa exclaimed as he circled the base of the tree.

The lowest branches were far above his head. Even standing on Garith's shoulders, he'd be unable to begin climbing. Why hadn't they thought to bring a rope with them?

"We'll have to come back," Garith was saying. "We can bring a rope tomorrow."

Raffa shook his head. Tomorrow might be too late for the little bat. He had to figure out a way to harvest the vine *now*.

A solution came to him. He hesitated for a moment, then decided to act before he could change his mind: He stripped off his tunic, took out his penknife, and began slicing the leather into strips.

"What are you doing?" Garith said, his eyes wide. "Aunt Salima's going to kill you!"

Raffa's tunic had been new that season. He had long wanted one like it. Years earlier, Salima had made one for Mohan and another for Ansel. Last winter Garith had received one as a birthday gift. Finally, this fall, it had been Raffa's turn.

Salima had tanned the deer hides herself, pieced them together, and painstakingly sewed the seams, reinforcing them with waxed thread. It was a beautiful tunic, sturdy and serviceable, with a hood and two large pockets. All of Salima's menfolk loved their tunics; Mohan's and Ansel's were by now nearly worn to rags.

"She'll understand," Raffa said, with more hope than certainty.

"Wait. . . . No. . . . Don't do it," Garith said in a monotone. "There. Now I can tell her that I tried to stop you. And don't you even think about touching mine."

It didn't take long for Raffa to cut up the whole tunic and tie the strips together firmly into a long rope. He found a rock the size of his two fists together and secured it to one end. Taking hold of the rope, he whirled the rock around his head, then let it fly experimentally.

"Hey—watch it!" Garith yelled as the rock whizzed past him.

"Sorry," Raffa said, and reeled the rock back in. "You'd better move."

After several tries, Raffa still hadn't managed to fling the rock over the lowest branch. "Oh, for quake's sake, let me try," Garith said. He tossed the kerchief to the ground and got to his feet.

He took up a stance a few yards away. Holding his

arm out away from his body, he whirled the rock and released it.

"*Ha!*" Garith shouted, and raised his arms in triumph as the rock soared over the branch on the first try.

It was no surprise to Raffa; Garith had always bettered him in athletic ability. Still, he couldn't resist a little jab. "Isn't luck a wonderful thing?" he said, and grinned when Garith pretended not to hear.

"Here, let me," Garith said, holding out his hand for the rope.

Raffa maneuvered the rope so it was positioned at the bole. "No, I want to do it," he said.

"But I'll be faster."

Garith was probably right, and Raffa wavered for a moment. Then he took firmer hold of the rope. "I saw it first," he said. He didn't add the real reason: that it was *his* mission to save the bat. His alone—not his father's, not Garith's.

"Oh, fine," Garith said. "But if you can't get it, you should come down and let me try."

That seemed fair enough, and Raffa nodded. Holding the rope with both hands and leaning backwards, he walked up the trunk and made it safely onto the first branch.

It took a while, but at last he hauled himself onto the third limb. He was now quite high above the ground. After a quick glance, he gripped the limb more firmly with his legs and resolved not to look down again. He wondered if Garith would have been nervous up here, too. Probably not, he thought with an inward sigh.

Raffa turned his attention to the vine. It had an abundance of small scarlet leaves.

"It's the right one!" he called down to Garith.

"Good," Garith called back. "So gather it and let's get out of here."

Raffa used the leather rope to tie himself to the branch. He held his knife in one hand and prodded the vine with the other.

A sharp burning sensation stung his fingers and shot all the way up his arm, shoulder, and neck—right into his brain. For a moment he saw red, as if fiery sparks were exploding inside his head.

"OUCH!" he yelled, and yanked his hand away.

"What's wrong?" Garith called from below. "Are you all right?"

Raffa blinked. He stared at his hand, then flexed his fingers. Nothing. No itching or burning or redness.

Bracing himself, he gingerly touched the vine again. This time, it felt . . . like a vine.

Could he have imagined the burning feeling? He frowned, thinking hard, until the realization came to him: The sting had been an intuition, like those he sensed when making botanical compounds. He had never before felt it on touching a plant.

Weird upon strange, he thought.

"Hi, my name's Garith. What's yours?" Garith shouted, clearly impatient.

"Sorry," Raffa called back. "It's fine. I'll be done in a minute."

He levered the knife under one end of the vine, then slid it gently along a section of the stem, keeping the blade hard against the branch's bark. With the end of the vine free, it was easy to unwind the rest of it and dislodge its roots from the mulch.

From his pocket he took a piece of cloth and wrapped the vine, then tucked the little parcel safely away. Before descending, he searched the trees nearby. He saw no other streaks of red. But at least he would know where to look next time—if indeed it was the right plant.

Raffa looped the rope over the branch on which he stood, and with a combination of sliding and hand-over-hand, he quickly dropped to the ground.

"Took you long enough," Garith said.

"Well, I got it, anyway," Raffa said. He glanced up at the sky. Not many of the sun's rays could penetrate the canopy, but those that did were angled low.

"Let's go," Garith said. "And keep your eyes open for lunatic owls."

CHAPTER SIX

IT was sunfall by the time the boys approached the cabin. Both of them raised their heads and sniffed the air as the house came into view.

"Meat?" Raffa said, puzzled and incredulous.

At the same moment, Garith said, "Do you smell meat?"

Most of Obsidia's populace subsisted largely on a diet of grains and vegetables. There were several types of grain crops, and vegetables grown in countless small holdings. Many families kept chickens for their eggs; milk and cheese and clabber could be bought at the market from the dairy farmers. Fisher folk seined the river and the

Vast, and brought their catch to market as well. But meat was reserved exclusively for special occasions. Despite their fatigue, the boys ran the last stretch of the path.

As curious as Raffa was about the meat, the little bat was foremost in his mind. When they reached the cabin, Garith headed around the side of the house to the back dooryard, as they usually did.

Raffa pulled up short. "You go on," he said. Without waiting for a reply, he entered the cabin through the little-used front door.

The box was where he had left it, on the corner shelf above the stove. Holding his breath, he moved it carefully to the table and lifted the rag.

The little bat lay there, limp and inert. Raffa saw no movement, not even in its tiny chest. He touched the bat's body with a trembling finger—and held it there gently in relief. The bat was still warm!

He moved his finger so he could feel the bat's heartbeat, although it was not so much a beat as the weakest of flutters.

The back door opened, and Mohan strode into the room. "Well?"

Raffa pulled the vine from his pocket. "Is this it?" he asked anxiously.

Mohan bent over and inspected the vine. "I think so," he said. "Mind you, I never saw it myself. But it fits the description."

Raffa watched closely as his father picked up the vine. He turned it in his hands to look at it from all angles, then began to speak. "The first thing—"

"I thought I would take some clippings first," Raffa said hurriedly. He knew it was rude to interrupt, but he wanted to do this work without his father's prompting.

He had thought about the vine the whole way home. Now he took a breath and spoke again before he lost his nerve. "Da? Could I— would you let me do this on my own? I'll say what I'm thinking, and if I'm right, I'll go ahead, but if I'm wrong, you could tell me?"

Mohan stared at him for a moment. Then he held out the vine with one hand. "As you wish," he said.

Raffa took the vine. He hesitated before speaking, wanting to be sure of his words in front of his father. "A hand's breadth per clipping," he said slowly, "and leave enough over to work with."

After snipping the vine into even lengths, he put each clipping in a jar of water. If the vine proved useful, the clippings would, with luck, grow to provide a continuing supply.

"It was living in shade. That means the north window." He took the jars two at a time and placed them on the window ledge.

Then he used a mortar and pestle to begin grinding the rest of the vine into a paste. He sniffed it curiously, but there was no strong odor.

"You said the child was badly burned, so to start with, your grandmother probably added it to the usual combination for burns." Raffa was talking more to himself than to his father. He found that speaking his thoughts aloud was actually helpful; it forced him to think more clearly. Besides which, if he viewed it as thinking aloud, he could almost pretend that Mohan wasn't there.

"So I'm going to try the combination I used already— the one for slashes, plus arnicullus, because of the owl, plus the vine."

He did not look at Mohan as he gathered the jars and utensils he needed. There was still a quantity of the poultice he had used on the bat earlier. He pounded the stem and leaves of the scarlet vine to a pulp, then added some to the poultice.

As he stirred, the paste began to take on a gentle vermilion glow, and in his mind he heard something that sounded like a faraway cowbell—not musical, but not unpleasant. He gave the paste several more turns with the pestle, then drew in his breath sharply. "Da, look," he said.

The paste was glittering and flashing in every shade of red. Sparks seemed to dance and move through the paste, keeping time with the gentle clinking in his inner ear. It was like nothing Raffa had ever seen before.

The paste glittered even more fiercely for a mere blink of time, then subsided to a dull glow again.

"Odd upon strange," Mohan said.

That was all he had to say. Raffa had hoped for at least a crumb of praise; he fought his disappointment by reminding himself that he didn't even really want his father there in the first place. He turned his attention to the bat, undoing the bindings, applying the new poultice, then rewrapping the wounds.

The next step was to make an infusion to feed to the bat. Raffa began work on this with no comment from his father. Normally with an unknown botanical, an apothecary would make several poultices before creating an infusion. It seemed that Mohan was willing to let Raffa skip several steps because the patient was a bat, not a person.

Raffa pondered for a few moments, then decided

to add the vine pulp to a standard combination used to stop bleeding. As he began to stir, his brain was assailed by a chaos of splotches and blots so ugly, it seemed to him that they even smelled bad.

"Wrong," he said hastily. Then he looked up at his father. "I mean, I changed my mind. I—I have a better idea." He knew that Mohan would not take kindly to any mention of an intuition.

He tried again, combining the vine with a solution of mummer petals and mellia, the usual ingredients for a strengthening tonic. This time when the vine pulp was stirred in, he experienced only a relaxed, tranquil feeling.

He often felt this when working with botanicals. It had nothing to do with his body; certainly his hands were always busy at such times. It was hard to describe—a silent but harmonious hum in his brain, not nearly as definite or dramatic as when he saw lovely colors or heard music. Before, with standard combinations, it had meant that he was close to an ideal mix. He hoped it meant the same thing now.

The infusion turned red and began to gleam. Now Raffa took up a tiny spoonful . . . and paused with the spoon held before him. It wasn't that he was afraid, but he had never before tested an unknown infusion. What if it burned his tongue? Or made him vomit, or—

Mohan stepped forward and held out his hand for the spoon.

"That is the correct procedure," he said. "But we don't know for certain that this is the right plant. If so, it is unusually powerful. You are not yet full grown, so the crucible is mine."

Emotions tumbled over each other in Raffa's mind: resentment at his father's interference, a flicker of relief at not having to taste the infusion, and then a blast of annoyance with himself for feeling relieved. Did this mean that he wasn't really ready to work on his own yet?

Lost for a moment in those thoughts, he gave a little start when he felt Mohan take the spoon from his fingers. His father put a few drops of the liquid on the tip of his tongue, then emptied the rest of the spoon's contents between his lower lip and gum.

Together they waited. Many harmful poisons were bitter on the tongue, and the human body would often begin rejecting the substance at the first taste of it, by producing a flood of saliva.

"A little bitter," Mohan pronounced. "But no more so than, say, any of the brassinels. I would guess that at the very worst, it's a cinder."

Raffa grinned in recognition of an old family joke. Cinder was a cat who had lived with them for several years. Named for the color of her fur, Cinder was a mild-tempered creature who possessed not the least shred of hunting instinct. The mice population in the house and yard had thrived during Cinder's tenure. One day she had wandered off and never returned.

In Raffa's family, a *cinder* was something at once both harmless and useless. Many plants growing in the wild were cinders; it was an apothecary's business to distinguish them from the useful and the harmful.

With a hollow reed, Raffa sucked up some of the infusion, using his tongue as a stopper to keep the liquid from draining out. He pried open the bat's tiny mouth, inserted the other end of the reed, and released the infusion. Then he gently held its mouth closed while he stroked its throat to make it swallow.

To his delight, he felt the bat's throat working under his finger. Only a little fluid trickled out of one side of its mouth. He dosed it again, then covered the bat and took it back to its warm corner.

"Heal, little bat," he whispered. "Please?"

CHAPTER SEVEN

RAFFA and Mohan stepped outside to join the others around the fire pit. Along with Ansel and Salima, Garith was admiring the roast of lamb whose drippings hissed and sizzled appetizingly.

Salima's smile of greeting quickly vanished as she tilted her head in puzzlement. "Raffa, where is your tunic?"

"Uh-oh," Garith said under his breath.

Raffa went back into the cabin and came out again with the coil of leather rope. He held it up wordlessly.

"Oh, Raffa," Salima said. "What happened?" She reached out and touched the leather sadly, as if saying good-bye to the tunic.

"Mam, it was for a good reason, I swear," Raffa said.

Salima's face was stern. "I don't doubt that," she said, "but deer hide is not easy to come by, and that tunic was a whole season's labor. I will be thinking of how you can work to help replace it."

"I'm sorry, Mam. Truly I am."

If there had been any other way, he would never have cut up his beloved tunic. While he hated disappointing his mother, he still did not regret what he'd done.

"We'll speak of it later," Salima said. "Now, all hands needed."

Mohan and Ansel moved the table and benches out into the yard. Garith hung green-glowing lanterns from the eaves. Their light source was an essence distilled from phosphorescent mushrooms, an invention of Salima's.

Raffa followed his mother's directions to set out every available trencher and bowl, then scattered flower petals and fragrant herbs on the ground around the table. His curiosity mounted: Why the celebration? He was glad for the distraction. Otherwise, he might have done nothing but worry about the bat.

When at last the family drew up to the table, the yard looked and smelled very festive. For the first several

minutes, there was no talk, only eating. Mohan carved
the roast into generous slices. Salima served Raffa's
favorite vegetable dish: shredded red cabbage simmered
in cider, with chunks of apples. There were biscuits, too,
instead of the usual bread. After their long and eventful
day, both boys were famished. Raffa ate twice of the
lamb and the cabbage.

With the sharpest pangs of hunger banished, the talk
began, Ansel speaking first. "So, how was your day in
the Forest?" he asked the boys.

"Something strange," Raffa answered.

"No, *two* somethings," Garith said.

Raffa cast a quick look at his cousin. He wanted his
parents and Uncle Ansel to know about the day's discoveries, but not that the owl had attacked them. Garith's
wound was hidden under his hair, and so far as Raffa
could tell, he hadn't mentioned it yet. If Mohan and
Salima found out, it would be a long time before Raffa
would be allowed to return to the Forest without them.

Garith caught his glance and gave him the tiniest of
nods. He went on to describe the clearing.

"The track went north, you say?" Mohan asked.

"Yes, and we tried to follow it but there was this
owl. . . ." Garith told how the bird had flown at them,

but he stopped short of saying that he had been attacked. Raffa looked away from him pointedly, which he knew Garith would take as a silent thanks.

Mohan looked sharply at Raffa. "The owl prevented you from following the track?"

"I didn't think of it at the time," Raffa said slowly, "but that's what it seems like—"

"Ridiculous," Ansel said. "Why ever would it do such a thing?"

"Perhaps its nest was somewhere nearby," Salima said.

Raffa remembered a time when he was much younger, playing in a meadow not far from the cabin. A partridge had burst forth in a flurry of feathers almost underneath his nose. Then it had staggered and flopped awkwardly a few feet away, dragging one wing. Certain that he could catch the injured bird, Raffa had chased it for a good few minutes, the bird continually flapping just out of reach. Then, suddenly, it had taken wing and soared over his head, clearly not the least bit injured. When he told his mother about it later, she had chuckled and said that the bird had feigned injury to lead him away from her nest. "She probably had either eggs or chicks," Salima explained, and Raffa had marveled at the bird's cleverness.

Now he frowned. "But it wasn't like that. I've never seen a bird act this way."

"Can birds get foaming sickness?" Garith asked.

Mohan shook his head. "Only fur-bearing animals get foaming sickness," he said. "I've never heard of birds getting anything like it."

Raffa could tell that both his parents were disturbed by the news about the clearing and the owl. But Uncle Ansel could contain himself no longer.

"Enough of such talk. Come now, appletip for everyone!" he boomed out. He poured for the adults, and then, with a wink at Salima, trickled the merest thread of appletip into the boys' water tumblers.

Then he stood and raised his drink. "To all of us . . ." He paused dramatically. *Soon to be residents of the Commons!"*

"What?" Garith exclaimed. "What are you talking about?"

Raffa glanced quickly at Mohan and Salima. His mother looked calm and unruffled, as she usually did, and his father's face was unreadable.

"An announcement today," Ansel said, "by two Commoners."

That explained the gathering in the square.

The Commoners were, logically enough, the people who held important jobs in the Commons, where the seat of Obsidia's government was located. Ansel sat down again but leaned toward the group, his voice growing louder and more excited with each word.

"They've decided to appoint official apothecaries—and both of our families have received invitations! Others will follow, but they wish us to be the first. We will live on the grounds of the Commons, and gardens will be planted exactly as we order."

His face was flushed with excitement. "A laboratory. And a glasshouse! Imagine being able to grow the tenderest plants the year round!"

"We'd live at the Commons?" Garith asked, his eyes glowing.

"In Gilden itself?" Raffa exclaimed.

His only visit to the city, two summers earlier, had been by far the most exciting few days of his life. With his parents and Garith's family, he had helped out at the apothecary booth of a grand summer fete. The fete itself was a raucous delight, with games and hawkers and performing troupes, but he had been even more impressed by the city's youngsters. They moved easily through the confusion of lanes and alleys and buildings and squares—on their own, with what seemed to be complete freedom from adult interference.

How small and quiet the settlement had seemed on their return! For weeks afterward, Raffa and Garith talked longingly of Gilden.

And now they would be going there to live!

"Truly?" Raffa squeaked in excitement.

Ansel laughed. "Well, I don't think your bed will be in the Advocate's quarters," he said. "But, yes, we will be housed in comfort, with all our meals provided."

Garith held his hands out toward Raffa, palms flat and together, and Raffa clapped his own hands with his cousin's between them, the usual gesture for celebration.

His mind raced ahead. Maybe he and Garith could have their own corner of the glasshouse. Maybe even a workspace in the laboratory, all to themselves! Raffa could already see himself in those splendid surroundings, and in that instant he knew exactly what he wanted to do there.

Experiment!

He could try out scores of new combinations. The possibilities were numberless. . . . Who knew what cures he might discover with everything he needed at hand, and the freedom to use it all?

Then Mohan cleared his throat, pulling Raffa out of his reverie. "Ansel, Garith," he said, his voice quiet but firm. "Salima and I are glad in your gladness, and we did not wish to spoil the celebration. But I have changed my mind. We will not be joining you. I have decided that we will remain here, in our home."

Silence fell over them like a shroud. Raffa sucked in his breath as his first feelings of bewilderment and disappointment dissolved into anger. How could Da have made such an important decision on his own? He should have talked it over with them—they should have decided as a family!

Raffa's anger grew thick as smoke, choking off any possibility of speech. He could feel Garith looking at him but refused to meet his gaze; he was angry at Garith, too. Which was unfair, but he couldn't help it. Why did Garith always get everything he wanted?

Uncle Ansel was on his feet again. "Mohan, I cannot believe it. How can it suit you to have your time taken up with every case of—of—boils and sore feet and reeking flatulence for miles around? With the resources of the Commons, you could achieve great good. Not just for a few patients, but for the world!"

He drew a breath in an attempt to calm himself. "And

if you will not think of yourself, then think of your son."

At these words, Raffa found himself wanting to duck under the table, as everyone's eyes were suddenly trained on him.

Ansel went on, "We all know of his abilities. Does he not deserve the best chance to hone his skills? His talent is wasted here!"

Raffa felt a great wave of warmth toward his uncle. But from the way Mohan was sitting, with his spine straight and his head proud, Raffa knew that Uncle Ansel had not swayed him.

"I do not think it ever a waste to help those in need of help," Mohan said at last. "Raffa will learn that here perhaps better than he could in Gilden."

Ansel turned to Salima. He was her older brother, but by little more than a year, and Raffa had always thought that his mother acted like the elder. "Sister, I beg you," he said, his voice quieter. He reached across the table for her hand. "I truly believe that this is our calling—what we are meant to do in this life. The chance to raise our art to its highest levels. How can we refuse?"

Raffa was watching his mother closely. When she lowered her eyes and did not speak, he dared to hope that her silence was because she did not want to take up against Mohan. If she wanted to go to the Commons, too—if they were all allied against him, maybe there was a chance. . . .

Ansel tried one last tactic. "Think of Garith," he said to Salima. "How could he do without you?"

Raffa saw his mother's eyes widen in hurt. Ansel had scratched at a scab that never truly healed: the death of Aunt Fleuria. Since Garith's birth, Salima had been the only mother figure he had ever known, and Raffa knew that she loved him as if he were her own son.

Then Salima's eyes narrowed. "It is *your* choice to take him away from here," she said. "Is it the best thing for him, do you think?" She did not raise her voice, but the words held a keen edge.

A few long moments of stillness. Then Garith burst out, "I'll be fine. It's not like I'm a baby or anything."

His words seemed to bring them back to themselves, the tension loosening all at once.

"It's getting late," Salima said, "and perhaps we've had more drink than is wise for serious talk. We can speak of this again another time."

Mohan went to see to the barn animals for the night. Ansel doused the fire in the pit. Raffa and Garith began to clear the table while Salima put the food away. The boys spoke in low tones.

"We need a plan," Raffa said, still envious of his cousin but no longer angry at him.

"To get him to change his mind," Garith agreed. "Let's both think on it. We'll figure something out. It might take a while, but sure upon certain we'll both be living in Gilden!"

Spurred by Garith's optimism, Raffa felt his spirits rise a tiny bit. Mohan had not returned by the time Ansel and Garith departed, and Raffa suspected it was deliberate avoidance on his father's part. Before getting ready for bed, he checked on the bat. It might have been his imagination or his hopes, but the bat now seemed to be asleep rather than unconscious, its breathing easier and more even.

Salima knelt for a moment by Raffa's pallet.

"Mam—"

"Not tonight," she said, her kiss to his forehead as firm as her voice. "It's been a long day."

Raffa expected to be kept awake by a welter of thoughts on everything that had happened. Instead, he fell asleep even before his mother left his side.

CHAPTER EIGHT

"Skee . . . skeeeee . . ."

Raffa was dreaming—a gray, shapeless dream. Out of the grayness came a single sound repeated over and over.

"Skeeee. Skeeee. SKEEEE!"

He sat up so suddenly that for a moment he felt dizzy, his pulse pounding in his ears. It was early morning. He was alone in the cabin, his parents already up and about. Then—

"SKEETO! SKEEEETO! SKEEEEETOOOO!"

It wasn't a dream. It sounded almost like words, in a voice between a rasp and a whisper. Not loud, but urgent, maybe even desperate. And it was coming from the box holding the bat.

Bats didn't sound like that. They squeaked and chittered, like mice. Raffa shook his head hard, trying to clear the fuzziness of sleep from his brain.

He waded on his knees to the end of his pallet. In the gloom of dawn it was hard to see, but he could make out the box on the corner shelf, same as it had been for two days now.

A tiny head popped up and peered over the edge of the box. Raffa let out a squawk of surprise and delight. A furry head with enormous ears. A little face with enormous eyes, which were fixed on him with a gaze steady as a moonbeam.

Raffa moved slowly, so as not to startle the little creature, and picked up the box, trying not to jar it. The bat's voice dropped again to a raspy whisper. "Skeeto, skeeto, skeeto . . ." This was followed by a few chitters and clicks.

Raffa carried the box to the table, then opened the cabin door for more light. Holding his breath, he looked inside the box.

The poultice was working! He could see that the bindings were clean and dry, which meant that no further blood or pus had seeped out during the night. After but a single application! It was truly astounding. His first thought was that he could hardly wait to show his father—but then he scowled. He was still angry at Mohan over his decision not to move to Gilden.

"Skeeto?"

Raffa shook his head, utterly bewildered. There was no question about it: The strange sound was definitely coming from the bat's mouth, but it wasn't a normal bat noise. Was it possible . . . Could the bat be *talking* to him?

"Nonsense," he said aloud, and forced his thoughts in a more practical direction. What should he do next? Water—it must be thirsty. He would give the bat a drink.

He bustled around the cabin, gathering up a hollow reed and a tumbler, pouring water from the kettle on the stove.

The bat had to be hungry, too, having not eaten in almost two days. He would need to catch some insects for it—

Insects?

Raffa dropped the kettle, which clattered to the floor. Eyes wide, he turned slowly to look at the bat again.

"Skeeto?" he whispered. "Are you trying to say . . .
mosquito?"

The bat seemed delighted. Eyes gleaming, it bobbed
up and down excitedly. "M'skeeee! M'skee—m'skee—
m'skeeeeeto!" Then, apparently exhausted by the effort,
it fell back onto its bed of milkweed fluff.

Raffa stood frozen before the table. Surely he wasn't
hearing things quite right. Somehow his brain was all
mixed up, making the bat's squeaks sound like words.

Steady on, he told himself. Back to the task at hand.
The bat needed to eat, and that meant insects.

He draped the rag loosely over the top of the box,
then went out into the yard. There would be flies in the
shed around Dobbles, their tricolored cart horse, but
catching crawling bugs would be quicker.

It took only a few minutes to gather several ants,
some wood lice, and a beetle that looked to be bigger
than the bat's mouth. To make it easier to feed the bat,
he crushed each bug as he caught it.

Back inside, he pinched a single ant between his
thumb and forefinger, then uncovered the box again.
The bat was as he had left it, on its back and moving
its legs feebly. It raised its head and opened its mouth
eagerly.

"Here you go," Raffa said. "A nice juicy ant." He dropped it into the bat's mouth.

The bat chewed once, swallowed, and immediately opened its mouth again. It ate seven ants and ten wood lice with barely a breath in between.

There was only one insect left.

"It's pretty big, this beetle," Raffa muttered, wondering if maybe he should feed it to the bat in smaller pieces. But before he could decide, the bat lunged for it and gulped it down.

Then it peered up at Raffa.

"Beetle," it said. "Big. Juicy."

Raffa felt as if he'd been sleepwalking and was now wide awake. The full realization of what was happening hit him like a cold slap. He backed away from the table slowly, then turned and ran out the door.

"*Da!*" he shouted. "DA, COME QUICKLY!"

Mohan stood beside Raffa looking down at the bat in its box. With what seemed to be equal curiosity, the bat stared up at them.

Mohan bent over for a closer look. The bat opened its mouth and—

Squeak. Chitter chitter click squeak.

Perfectly normal bat sounds. Raffa felt his face growing hot. "What do you mean, '*Squeak*'?" he said to the bat. "You—you weren't squeaking a few minutes ago. You were talking about the beetle!" He turned to Mohan. "Da, I swear I wasn't imagining things."

"Healers often develop very close bonds with their patients," Mohan said. "It would not surprise me at all if that is what has happened here."

Raffa felt a pulse of pleasure at his father calling him a healer. It was almost the opposite of being called a garbler. At the same time, it was clear that Mohan hadn't believed him. "I know what you mean, Da, but it really was talking."

Mohan looked at him sternly. "Too much imagination can be dangerous in a healer," he said.

The heat of frustration rose in Raffa's face. He hated making a fool of himself in front of his father. He knew he hadn't imagined it, but if the bat wouldn't talk now, how could he prove it?

"Just say one word," he begged the bat. "Say 'beetle.' Or 'mosquito.' Remember? 'Skeeto'?"

"Never mind," Mohan said. "What is important is the healing." He reached into the box and gently fanned out the bat's left wing, the one that had been so badly torn. "I've never seen anything like this."

For the moment, Raffa stifled his dismay. When Mohan tried to open the other wing, still bound with matchsticks, the bat hissed and bared its teeth.

"I didn't put any poultice on that wing," Raffa said, "only on the other one. Do you think it might also help heal bone breaks?"

"It is worth the attempt," Mohan answered. "If nothing else, it might ease the pain there."

Raffa fetched the remaining vine paste, scooped up a bit on his fingertip, then bent over the box.

The bat opened its wing.

Mohan smiled. "It seems you've made a friend. Or at least, as I said, a strong connection to the creature."

As Raffa gently applied the poultice, the bat half-closed its eyes and made a low purring sound.

Mohan was watching closely. "We'll be wanting to work with that vine," he said. "We must see to the care of the clippings."

Raffa picked up the rag coverlet. "You should sleep now, little bat," he said. "It will help you get better faster."

"*S-s-sleep.*"

Raffa's mouth fell open. Mohan's head jerked up in surprise.

The bat gazed at them, then focused squarely on Raffa.

"*Sleep,*" it said clearly. And then, "*Perch?*"

CHAPTER NINE

WITH the bat asleep, Mohan called Salima from her work in the garden. She joined them at the table. Mohan was hunched over, his elbows on his knees. He nodded at Raffa.

"Mam, the bat—" Raffa paused, aware of how improbable his next words would sound. "The bat *talked*."

Salima cast a quick look at him, then at Mohan. It was readily apparent from their expressions that Raffa had spoken the truth. She glanced briefly at the bat's box before returning her gaze to Raffa.

"The bat . . . talked," she repeated slowly.

A long moment of silence. Long enough that Raffa began to feel itchy.

"So," Salima said at last, "what did it say?"

Raffa let out a bark of laughter; he couldn't help it. Even Mohan's lips twitched a little.

"I wasn't trying to be funny," Salima objected.

"Sorry," Raffa said. "He asked for mosquitoes. He said other things as well, like *perch* and—and I can't remember what else."

He could feel excitement bubbling through him. This was surely the most astounding thing that had ever happened—not just to him or his family but to any apothecary anywhere!

His thoughts whirled with possibilities. Talking pets! Farm animals that could tell their owners helpful things! Working beasts, like horses and sheepdogs . . . if they could talk, how much easier to train and direct them!

And beyond that, there was the vine itself. If indeed it had made the bat talk, what else might it be capable of? Raffa could hardly wait to test it in various combinations—to unlock what was sure to be its amazing potential.

But Mohan was staring down at his hands, clearly not feeling even a shred of excitement. "I do not know what this is, Raffa," he said gravely.

Raffa was bewildered by his father's gloom. He turned to Salima, who held up her hand in anticipation of his question.

"It's . . . impossible," she said. "And yet it happened. When people hear of it—I'm afraid—"

"Your mother is right," Mohan snapped. "If word spreads that an infusion is responsible, there will be no end to the ridiculous demands that will besiege us. And the garblers will multiply like flies."

He stood and jabbed at the fire with the poker. "There is too much we do not know. Was it even the infusion in the first place? If it was, will there be unwanted effects, and can we create an antidote? Would it have the same result with all creatures? How will it affect humans?"

He raised the poker in warning. "I truly fear what might happen if someone without scruples were to discover this. Knowledge without wisdom can be worse than dangerous. Tell no one, Raffa, about the vine, and especially about the bat, until we've had a chance to study further."

Raffa nodded solemnly. It made him feel important, to be guarding an apothecarial secret. At the same time, he chafed at his father's caution. But at least Mohan saw the importance of experimenting with the vine.

"One more thing, Raffa," his mother said. "You should take care with your little bat. There are those who would think to profit from such a wonder. They would not hesitate to take him from you by stealth or even by force."

Raffa gasped. It hadn't occurred to him that someone might try to steal the bat! He cast a worried look at its box, then sat up straighter as his concern turned into resolve. No one was going to take the bat from him. He would do everything in his power to protect the little creature.

Mohan returned the poker to its holder. The family discussion was over for the time being. "We can begin to work with the vine," he said, "as soon as you finish mucking the vegetable beds."

That was all Raffa needed to hear. He spent the whole day in the garden, mucking with all his might.

Garith did not come by; Raffa suspected it was because his cousin and uncle were preparing for the move to Gilden. Busy as he was caring for the bat, Raffa hadn't thought of a way to convince his father to change his mind about living at the Commons. He wondered if

Garith had come up with an idea.

Later that evening, the bat awoke in a frenzy of hunger. Raffa was overjoyed: Hunger meant that the bat was healing. But the good news meant a great deal of work. He could hardly believe the amount such a small creature could eat.

He spent a full hour running back and forth from yard to house, catching insects and feeding them to the bat. When at last the little creature stopped opening its mouth the instant after swallowing, he plopped down on his pallet, exhausted.

"Whew," he said.

"Whew?" the bat said, and blinked a few times.

Raffa peered closely at the little bat's face. Its eyes were a smoky gray color, with a striking tinge of purple. All this time, he had thought that the bat's eyes were black; it was strange that he hadn't noticed before.

He wasn't sure how to talk to a bat. Not like a baby—this bat was fully grown, and he knew that bats could live several decades. The bat might well be older than he was.

He decided to try an experiment. Glancing around the room, he said the first three words that popped into his head. "Lantern, pallet, table."

Silence.

"Rucksack, bench, blanket."

More silence.

"Bucket, jug, water."

"Water?" the bat chirped. "Thirsty. Need water."

Raffa got up to fetch a reed and gave the bat a drink, thinking all the while. The bat had ignored every word except for *water*. Maybe that meant he could speak words for the things that bats knew, which would make complete sense. Why would a bat need to know what a bucket was?

"Name," Raffa said hesitantly. "Do you have a name?"

Silence again, but the bat was watching him intently. So he pointed to himself. "Raffa," he said. "My name is Raffa."

"Raffa," the bat said.

"Good!" Raffa was delighted. "If you need me, call out 'Raffa' and I'll come, okay?"

"Good! Raffa good!"

Raffa laughed, although he still wasn't sure how well the bat had understood him. "Well, at least now I've got a name for you," he said. "I'm going to call you Echo."

* * *

That first evening of Echo's recovery, Raffa learned that he had guessed correctly: The bat's vocabulary revolved for the most part around bat things. Raffa was delighted by the vast number of insects Echo could name. Gnat, moth, fluttereen, skimmer, wasp, pollenux, hornet, midge, starfly—there didn't seem to be a single flying insect Echo didn't know.

But Echo did not always speak when spoken to. Was it because the ability was so new and strange? Or was it his character? Grogginess especially seemed to affect him. On first waking, he made only bat sounds. Maybe it was the equivalent of Salima's incoherent grumbles in the morning before she'd had her first cup of tea.

Raffa fashioned a perch from a twig fastened to a leather thong, cut from the rope that had been his tunic. Once Echo was well enough to leave the box, he planned to wear him like a necklace. It was the best way he could think of to keep Echo safe.

He could hardly wait to introduce Echo to Garith. In his mind he tried out various scenarios. Should he go for the most dramatic effect? Or would it be better if he acted casually? In any case, he'd have to make sure he was in just the right position to see Garith's face when Echo spoke!

But the next day, when Garith and Ansel arrived in the afternoon, Echo was asleep. Mindful of what had happened when Mohan first met the bat, Raffa was not going to risk the chance that a groggy Echo would refuse to speak in front of Garith. It would make him look—and feel—like a complete fool.

He was willing to wait for exactly the right moment: He and Echo would put on a dazzling display, and Garith would be beyond astonished. Raffa would make sure to arrange things so that Uncle Ansel could be there, too.

He contented himself with showing Garith how well the bat's injuries were improving. Without waking Echo, he pointed out the rapidly healing scars on the bat's back and head. "And his wings are getting better, too," he said. "If he wakes up later, I can show you."

"That's amazing," Garith said. "Better than anything we've ever used! What were the combinations?"

Raffa told him, then added, "But you can't tell anyone else. Da says we need to work more with the vine. Shame upon sorry we have so little of it."

Garith went to the window to examine the clippings while Raffa returned the bat's box to the shelf. He took a few moments to fluff up the bedding, pleased that the bat was sleeping so restfully.

"Let's tell my father about this," Garith said. "I'm sure he'll want to know."

He headed for the door, with Raffa behind him. Then Garith halted abruptly and raised a hand, gesturing for silence.

The adults were standing in a corner of the yard. Mohan's voice was raised in anger. "—without even knowing what kind of project it is!"

"I told you already, I'll learn more on our arrival," Ansel responded. "The Chancellor herself wants to meet with me. And with you, too, if only you would change your mind!"

"But why would they not tell you more? Why all the mystery? I can make no sense of it, Ansel, and it worries me."

"Always the worrier! Why can you not see the good of this?" Ansel pounded his fist against something wooden, which made both boys jump.

There was a moment of heavy silence, and then Mohan sighed. "At least promise me this," he said. "That you will keep your eyes wide and your mind clear, so you might perceive things that are not what they seem."

Ansel mumbled a reply.

"Please, let's not argue on the day of your parting," Salima begged.

Raffa poked his cousin, and the boys drew back from the doorway.

"Today?" he said in dismay. "You're leaving today?"

"I know, it's happening awfully fast, isn't it?" Garith said. "Not today, but tomorrow morning early."

Raffa was shocked. He hadn't thought it would be so soon! How was it possible that Garith would no longer have lessons with him? That if he walked to the Vales' cabin, as he had countless times over the years, he would find it empty? He might even miss the way Garith always pinched his feet as they slept head to toe whenever they shared a bed.

"You'll come see me, won't you?" Garith said. "Get your parents to bring you for a visit as soon as you can. I won't know anybody there at first, except for my da, and he doesn't really count." He laughed, but without his usual ease, and it surprised Raffa to see him looking anxious.

For a moment, Raffa felt peeved. He was the one being left behind—why should Garith need comforting? But Mohan's decision was hardly Garith's fault.

"It's Gilden," he said, reaching up to rap Garith's

noggin playfully. "*Hundreds* of people live there, and surely at least one or two of them are either softhearted or dull-witted enough to become friends with you."

"Why, thank you, dear cousin," Garith replied, crossing his eyes.

Raffa laughed, and Garith joined in.

"Really, I expect you'll be so busy at first, you won't have time to worry about anything," Raffa said. His wistfulness returned as he thought of the glasshouse and the laboratory where Garith would be working.

"You're probably right," Garith said. "I mean, of course you're right—you're the baby genius!"

Raffa chased him out the cabin. That was their farewell, for Garith ran from the yard and kept on running. Neither of them said good-bye.

It was better that way.

CHAPTER TEN

RAFFA stared at the list that Mohan had chalked on the worktable's surface. There were more than three dozen combinations for poultices and two dozen for infusions, all standard preparations.

"We need a list of the vine's capabilities," Mohan said, "but we cannot work with it until the clippings have begun to grow. In the meantime, there is plenty to do. We'll begin by making fresh batches of these combinations. They're the ones I want to try first with the vine added. By the time they've been completed, the clippings should be ready to use."

It made perfect sense. Raffa wished it didn't. He could

have made most of these combinations in his sleep, but still his father checked on him frequently as he worked. "Take care," Mohan said. "Mistakes are seldom made with unusual combinations, for they receive our keenest attention. Carelessness with simple preparations is by far the greater danger."

The tasks were endless. Raffa fetched and carried. He stripped an infinite number of leaves from their stems and picked off twice that many flower petals. He washed the soil from roots and tubers until the skin on his fingers puckered. He sliced and chopped, peeled and pounded, scraped and grated—his knuckles as well as whatever he was holding.

Some good came out of all the work: It enabled him to fill his own jars with fresh ingredients. And he was too busy to miss Garith very much. During the long hours of drudgery, he had Echo to keep him company.

The bat continued to improve. The broken wing bones had knitted cleanly, and it was a happy day when Echo took flight again, a short staggering hop from the box to Raffa's arm.

Raffa began rising to start work before daybirth, when Echo was still awake. The bat would flit from shelf to ceiling to table edge, landing upside down or sometimes sidewise. Raffa continued talking through the steps of his work, but now with Echo listening.

"This is dried yarrow," Raffa said. "See these flower heads? I have to pick off every one of them, without getting any leaves mixed in. Like this."

"Raffa good!" the bat chirped, a phrase he repeated often.

Toward midmorning, he would alight on the perch necklace and go to sleep for several hours. It comforted Raffa to feel the bat's warmth on his chest.

Echo spoke more words every day. One evening, as he returned from devouring dozens of the moths that hovered around the lanterns in the yard, he tried to land on the perch. But with his left wing badly scarred, his flight was erratic: He missed the twig and grabbed the leather thong instead—along with a little of the skin on Raffa's neck.

"Ouch!" Raffa said. He unhooked the bat's claws gently and directed him to the twig.

"Ouch," an upside-down Echo said happily. "Ouch!"

And from then on, Echo called out "Ouch!" whenever he flapped in for a landing.

When he wasn't busy preparing combinations, Raffa had another job to do. True to her word, Salima assigned him the making of a new tunic. He had learned to knit when he was younger, producing several wobbly-edged scarves. For the tunic, his mother inspected his work often, and when it did not meet her standards, she made him rip it out and do it again. There were times when Raffa thought the garment would never be completed. It would be a cold winter with no tunic.

But Salima helped with the trickier parts, and when every last loose end had been securely woven in, Raffa was proud of his work. The wool was soft and thick and tightly knit; it would keep him warm even when wet. Now he had both tunic and rope, although he would never have shared that satisfaction with his mother.

Mohan had undertaken the care of the clippings. One morning, he called Raffa to the window ledge and handed him one of the jars.

"It's not growing," Mohan said.

Raffa examined the clipping. It seemed healthy enough, the stem firm, the leaves neither limp nor shriveled. Oddly, though, only a single tiny, wispy rootlet protruded from the end in the water, and there was no new growth at the other end.

"I cannot explain it," Mohan said. "I asked your mother yesterday; she could not fathom it, either."

Raffa returned the jar to its place on the ledge. He looked at each of the other jars and frowned.

"Did you do something with one of them?" he asked.

Mohan returned the frown. "Other than to tend them? No, why?"

"I took six clippings," Raffa said. There were only five jars on the sill.

Garith.

Raffa knew at once and beyond doubt that it was his cousin who had stolen the clipping. He felt torn between disappointment and irritation. Why hadn't Garith asked? Perhaps he had felt entitled to one, since he had gone to the Forest with Raffa. But he still should have asked.

Mohan too appeared to have guessed where the sixth clipping had gone, for he shook his head before speaking. "I know you want to work with the vine," he said, "so we'll begin. But we will use only two of the clippings. We must continue to try to grow the other three."

Being limited to just two clippings would restrict the number of experiments that could be done. To stretch the amount of vine pulp as far as possible, only small quantities would be used. Mohan decided to begin by testing if the vine could improve the poultice for rashes, among the most common of maladies.

Raffa pounded the scarlet vine eagerly. He took a small spoonful of a standard combination for rashes and added an even smaller amount of the pulp. As his hand stirred, his mind waited.

A tiny pinch, so quick he wasn't sure it had happened at all. Not comfortable, but not exactly painful, either— like a flick or a nudge . . .

He stood very still for a moment longer. Nothing more. He'd probably imagined it, and decided to move on. He couldn't wait to find out what would happen.

"Da, can I test it myself?"

No answer, so Raffa rushed into the silence. "On the back of my hand." He'd skip the blue-veined cheeks today, please upon thank you.

Mohan nodded. Raffa rubbed in a dab of poultice no larger than a kernel of wheat. The skin there immediately began to tingle and redden.

After a moment, the back of his hand started to itch. Raffa frowned and raised his hand off the tabletop to examine it more closely.

Now his hand was feeling warm . . . and warmer still. He sucked in his breath between his teeth. Mohan heard him and stepped around the table to take a look.

They watched in alarm as the skin on Raffa's hand

began to crack in several places. Layer after layer, the cracks were working their way down, the edges curling a little to reveal the tender pink flesh underneath.

"Wash it off—quickly," Mohan said.

Raffa ran to the bucket by the hearth and plunged his hand into it. Under the water, he rubbed at the cracks in mild panic.

"Ow—YOW!"

As his father rushed to his side, Raffa yanked his hand from the bucket. He cried out in horror. Instead of washing away the poultice, the water had spread its effects: Cracks were now splitting the entire back of his hand!

His skin felt like it was on fire. "Da—YOW, it hurts, it hurts!" He shook his hand hard, as if trying to fling away the pain. Instead, his action fanned the flames.

"Don't touch anything!" Mohan strode across the room and flung open the trapdoor to the cellar. He descended and was back moments later. Urgently but with precision, he quickened the combination for pernicious reactions and applied it to Raffa's hand.

Raffa could hardly wait for the combination of brightweed and ragged-jack to begin working. He knew what it would feel like, cool and soft and soothing. . . .

He gritted his teeth and began counting, trying to take his mind off the pain.

"One, two, three—"

By the time he reached ten, involuntary tears of pain were rolling down his cheeks.

"It's not working," Mohan said grimly.

"Da," Raffa gasped. It was hard to speak; he had to force out the words between bursts of what felt like flames on his hand. "The vine. Add it."

Mohan raised his eyebrows, but he moved at once to put a spoonful of the vine pulp into the brightweed combination. With his good hand, Raffa took up the pestle and began to turn.

"Again," Raffa panted. Mohan dropped more pulp into the mortar. Raffa turned the pestle again, and the paste glittered crazily in red.

Raffa dropped the pestle as the pain nearly overcame him. Mohan grabbed the mortar, took a hurried swipe of the paste, and smeared it on the back of Raffa's hand.

The result was as dramatic as a flood in a fireplace. Raffa let out a yowl crossed with a sigh, so great was his relief. He rubbed in more of the soothing poultice. Together he and Mohan saw the cracks begin to subside. After a third application, they vanished. A reddish cast to Raffa's skin was all that remained.

His legs weak and wobbly, he collapsed onto the bench. Mohan, too, settled himself heavily. Both were breathing hard.

"Powerful," Mohan rasped. "Even more than I had remembered."

If the cracks had gone any deeper, they might have begun bleeding badly. Raffa knew then how lucky he had been with the poultice and infusion for Echo. No, *lucky* wasn't the right word. He had heard the cowbell-like sound for the poultice, and sensed the silent hum of serenity for the infusion. That tiny pinch he'd felt moments ago—he shouldn't have ignored it, no matter how Da felt about intuitions.

He could not make the same mistake again; if he did, the consequences might be far more serious.

Mohan picked up the mortar—rather gingerly, Raffa thought—and carefully scraped its contents into the fire. "We'll work no more with the vine today," he said. "And from now on, I will do all the testing."

"But Da—!"

"Not another word," Mohan said, his voice stone and ice.

Raffa knew better than to talk back to that voice. He

went rigid with anger. The cracks had frightened him badly, and he needed another chance. Why couldn't his father understand that?

If he lost his nerve now, he might never find it again.

CHAPTER ELEVEN

GARITH.

Raffa sat up on his pallet in the gray of dawn. He had been dreaming again, or perhaps less than half awake. That tiny pinch had grown steadily stronger, more and more painful. He had twisted and squirmed in his sleep, trying to escape it, but it gripped tighter still, until it felt as though his very mind was cracking just as his skin had. . . .

And then he had woken thinking of Garith.

Raffa grabbed his tunic and pulled it on right over his nightclothes. He shoved his feet into his boots, sockless, and ran out of the cabin. He found Mohan in the shed, pitching fresh straw into Dobbles's stall.

"Da! Da, Garith—the clipping—"

"A steady morning to you, too," Salima interrupted him.

Raffa was startled; he hadn't noticed his mother there. Now he saw that she was sitting on a stool, cutting up carrots for the horse's breakfast.

Salima had been away from home the day before, attending a young woman in the settlement who was expecting her first child. At supper, Raffa and Mohan had told her about the misadventure with the vine.

"Mam, Da," Raffa said. "Garith has that clipping of the vine, and we have to tell him about what happened to my hand."

"I didn't know he had a clipping," Salima said, frowning.

"We realized it only yesterday," Mohan said.

"Could we send them a message?" Raffa asked.

There were limited choices for having a message sent from the settlement to Gilden. The message could be given to a courier, or to someone who was traveling there. Couriers cost money. A random traveler might not be reliable. A few families in the settlement kept messenger pigeons, which were the fastest way to send word but cost even more than a courier.

Mohan leaned on the handle of the hayfork, his forehead furrowed in thought. "They have only the one clipping," he said slowly, and was silent for a few moments.

Then he raised his head. "I am sure Ansel would do as we have done and attempt to grow the clipping before using it." His voice was stronger now. "He would not use the sole specimen."

A pause. "I hope you're right," Salima said.

"But it's not just Uncle Ansel we have to worry about!" Raffa blurted out. "What about Garith?"

"Garith would know as well," Mohan said. "I gave you boys a lesson on untried botanicals not long ago. Have you forgotten already? It included the necessity of growing clippings."

"But, Da, I showed him how well the bat's wounds have healed and he was really excited about it. He might want to try it as soon as he can—"

"Do you really think so little of your cousin? And for that matter, of my teaching?"

Flustered, Raffa couldn't think how to respond. This wasn't about Da's teaching—it was about Garith, his boldness and impulsiveness.

"Even if Garith should prove to be as irresponsible as you seem to think," Mohan went on, "his father will keep him from harm."

For an instant, Raffa tried to suppress his frustration. But he failed, and the words exploded. "Uncle Ansel doesn't watch over Garith every single second the way you do with me!"

Raffa was shocked at himself. When he dared to look at his father, Mohan's expression was thunder and magma, quake and storm, the angriest Raffa had ever seen him.

"You will never again speak to me with such disrespect." His father growled out the words one at a time.

Another silence.

Raffa swallowed hard, holding back tears. "I'm sorry, Da," he whispered.

He wasn't sorry for what he had said but for the way he had said it. He knew that he had ruined any chance for a calm future discussion of the subject.

Mohan began pitching hay again, his movements stiff with obvious anger.

Then Salima got to her feet. "Not the most enjoyable way to begin the day," she said. "Here is my proposal: When I go to the settlement this morning, I will make inquiries. If someone we know is traveling to the Commons, I will give them a message for Ansel, that the vine should be handled with particular care."

"And Garith," Raffa added in a small voice. "Please, Mam, be sure to say that the message is for Garith, too."

He left the shed, his shoulders slumped in defeat.

The day had never seemed so long as Raffa awaited his mother's return from the settlement. What if she had been unable to find anyone going to Gilden—what would he do then? He avoided his father altogether, even mulching the herb beds to stay busy outside the cabin.

The sole bright spot was Echo. After Raffa cleaned off his boots in the dooryard, he sat down on the bench and blew gently on Echo's face, which he had learned was the best way to wake the bat. Echo opened his eyes and looked up—or down, as he hung inverted on his perch. He studied Raffa's glum face closely.

"Raffa no good," Echo said.

Surprised, Raffa couldn't help his first smile of the day. Clearly, Echo *did* understand the words he used. Not only that, he seemed to know how Raffa was feeling.

Raffa stroked the bat gently. "I'm okay, Echo. I just have a lot on my mind."

"Skeeto," Echo said firmly. "Echo no good, eat skeeto, Echo good. Raffa eat skeeto, Raffa good."

Which made Raffa laugh. "I don't think that would work for me," he said. "But it's nice of you to think of it."

Raffa was pacing in the shed when Salima arrived home. He helped her put up the horse and cart. Then she nodded at him.

"Mannum Zimmer is traveling to Gilden," she said. "He has agreed to convey a message to my brother."

"When?" Raffa asked.

A pause. "In a week's time."

"A week?" Raffa said, aghast. "Mam, that's too long! We have to get the message to them sooner!"

Salima put her hands on his shoulders. "Raffa, I share your concern for Garith. But I had one other thought that put my mind at more ease. Both Ansel and Garith have surely been very busy settling in and learning their new duties. Neither of them will have the leisure for experimenting."

What Mam said made sense. But Raffa could not shake the feeling of dread from the dream he'd had, and he knew that neither of his parents would consider it a good reason for his continued worry. They had left him no choice. . . .

Salima pulled him closer and spoke quietly into his hair. "As for your disagreement with your father, I would ask you to consider that it is not an easy thing being a parent. None of us is perfect. Not even your beloved uncle."

Raffa put his arms around her waist. "I know no one is perfect, Mam. But sometimes you come quite close." He gave her a hug, in affection but also because he didn't want her to see the guilt on his face over what he was planning.

She pushed him away playfully, and he saw that she looked pleased. "Enough of your flattery," she said. Then, "Mannum Zimmer will reach the Commons in good time, Raffa. You need not trouble yourself over this further."

Raffa nodded at her reassuringly. He wasn't troubled any longer. He had made up his mind.

Raffa lay on his pallet, his body tight with tension. It felt like half the night was gone by the time he heard Mohan's snores and Salima's even breathing. He sat up slowly, cautiously, and listened again to be sure they were both asleep.

Earlier, he had surreptitiously packed his rucksack,

then hidden it in the shed. Mortar and pestle. Spoons and tongs. As many of his jars as he could carry—combinations, essences, and especially the ones containing Echo's treatments. A few clean rags. The leather rope. His waterskin. Some oatcake, apples, nuts, a round of cheese . . .

Everything he would need for a trip to Gilden.

The hard part would be getting out of the house without waking either parent. Raffa picked up his shoes, then took a deep, silent breath and held it. Willing himself not to look toward the alcove where his parents slept, he headed straight for the door. Its leather hinges made no sound as he slipped out. He tiptoed across the yard.

Dobbles nickered when Raffa entered the stall, but he was ready for that and fed the horse a handful of oats. Then he chalked a quick note on the wall of the shed:

Gilden, to see Garith. Home soon, don't worry!

Leaving word in the shed would let them know where he had gone before they'd had a chance to miss him. Of course, on seeing the note, they *would* worry. But the earliest ferry they'd be able to board was the evening one, and if all went well, they would receive a message from him long before that.

Raffa pictured himself arriving in Gilden on the morning ferry. At the Commons, he would find Garith perfectly well, and would warn him off using the vine. Uncle Ansel would send a pigeon to his parents telling them of his safe arrival—and inviting him to stay in Gilden for a while. A chance to see the new apothecary quarter . . . a few days on his own, away from his father's constant oversight . . . Raffa couldn't help a moment of wishfulness.

But that wasn't why he was going, he reminded himself stoutly. After he put on his shoes and shouldered his rucksack, he went around behind the shed and lit a lantern.

Echo was somewhere outside feeding. As Raffa had hoped, moths were soon drawn to his lantern light, followed shortly by a small hungry bat.

"Raffa not sleep!" Echo squeaked in surprise. His eyes were wide, their purple sheen glowing.

"Not tonight," Raffa whispered. He gave the bat a few minutes to feed, then held out the perch.

"Come, Echo," Raffa said, his voice low.

"Ouch," Echo said as he alit on the twig. He chittered with excitement, clearly delighted that Raffa was up and about at that hour.

Raffa tucked the necklace, bat and all, down the front of his tunic, and hurried off toward the road.

PART II

CHAPTER TWELVE

REACHING the southern ferry landing on foot took Raffa a good few hours. He had never walked anywhere near this distance in the dark before or, for that matter, by himself. But what could have been a spooky and unnerving trip was made interesting and fun because of Echo.

Echo periodically left the perch and flitted away to feed. The first time he returned, he began telling Raffa about his meal.

"Midge," Echo said. "Midge midge midge. Midge midge midge midge midge—"

Raffa laughed. "Echo, you don't have to tell me

about every single one you ate. I'll just assume it was a lot, okay?"

To light his way, Raffa had fashioned a torch of sorts: a rag tied to a stick. The rag had been soaked in the same distillation of phosphorescent fungi that was used in his family's lanterns. The glow lit his path only a few feet in front of him, but it was comforting all the same. And the track from the settlement to the ferry landing was clear and broad; he was in no danger of losing his way. He saw not a single soul during the entire walk.

Raffa arrived at the bank of the Everwide shortly before daybirth. The landing area was deserted. He found a space between a stack of crates and a piling, and sat down there to wait. As the sky lightened, the shapes around him took on form and detail: the ferry itself, smaller boats docked nearby, a small makeshift hut at the entrance to the pier—

With a groan, Raffa smacked himself on the head. The hut was for the fare collector: He would have to pay to board the ferry. In the stealth and haste of his departure, he hadn't thought of this.

Raffa had no money of his own and would never have dared to steal any from his parents. It was bad enough venturing out in the middle of the night without their knowledge or permission. He might be disobedient, but he was no thief.

"What am I going to do, Echo?"

Raffa's initial dismay quickly turned to anger at himself. A fine thing it would be to go skulking home without even having made it across the river!

"Raffa good?" Echo chirped.

"No, I'm not," he answered crossly.

"Raffa eat," Echo suggested.

"Is that your answer to everything?" he snapped.

Echo was silent. Raffa felt bad for taking out his anger on the bat. "I'm sorry, Echo," he said, scratching the bat behind the ears. "But eating won't fix this."

"Raffa *drink*," the bat said. "Raffa drink, Raffa good."

Raffa started to laugh, but the laugh got caught in his throat. Echo's words had given him an idea.

The sky turned from gray to rose and yellow as Raffa made his preparations. He finished by unfolding a clean rag and putting breakfast on it—an oatcake, an apple, and some shelled walnuts. Then he called Echo to his perch and tucked the bat down his tunic again.

He was ready.

Raffa saw a man hurrying up the road. His cap was

askew, his unlaced boots flapped on his feet, and he was struggling into his uniform jacket as he ran. It looked as though he was coming straight from his bed.

Seated now in plain sight on the edge of the dock, Raffa swung his legs in what he hoped was a carefree manner. He swallowed hard to quell his nervousness.

"Steady morning to you!" he called out as the man approached.

Raffa was pleased with himself; his voice had been cheerful and sure. Like Garith's. That was the secret, he told himself—he should act like Garith.

"Not for me," the man replied, then rolled his bloodshot eyes. "I was out late, and morning came as a rude shock. But the job's the job, so here I am to collect the fares."

"Would you like some breakfast?" Raffa said.

The man looked surprised. "You'd share yours?"

"Sure," Raffa said. "My mam packed me a full tucker for the trip." He broke the oatcake in two and held out half on his flat palm.

The man took the cake and nodded his thanks. "Going to Gilden, then?"

"My first time on my own," Raffa said. "I have some botanica to deliver." He patted his rucksack.

He had decided that the best strategy was not to stray too far from the truth. A complicated lie might trip him up.

"Will there be a lot of people traveling today?" he asked.

The guard shook his head. "Not on the first crossing," he said. "Too early for most. You'll probably be the only one."

Raffa frowned. "If it's just me, will the ferry go across?"

"Oh, course it will. No worries there. Most times, the dawn boat crosses empty. See, the rafts dock for the night on this side of the river, so there's always a boat goes over first thing, to fetch them that wants from the Gilden side."

One less thing to fret about. Raffa took out his waterskin. "Would you like a drink?" he asked, trying to keep his voice light. "It's sweet cider, made from our own apples."

The man hesitated. "I shouldn't be taking all your food," he said. "What would your mam think of me?"

Raffa felt a momentary pang over having to scheme against the man, who seemed a good sort. But he had to get to Gilden, had to stop Garith from doing something foolhardy with the vine. His resolve strengthened.

"She'll never know, will she?" He gave the man what he hoped was a rakish wink.

The man eyed the waterskin longingly, then grinned at Raffa. "My mouth is sour dry," he said. "A drink would do me a world of good."

"Help yourself," Raffa said.

The man uncorked the waterskin and took a quick swig. "Delicious," he said, wiping his mouth with the back of his hand.

"You'd be doing me a favor if you drank some more," Raffa said. "Full up, it's heavy."

"In that case, I consider it my duty to come to a traveler's aid!" The man laughed, and Raffa joined in with a forced chuckle. He hadn't realized before that it wasn't easy to fake a laugh.

The man tipped his head back and gulped down the cider. "Ah! That's steady upon solid." He handed the waterskin back to Raffa. "Best breakfast I've had in months. I'm a better man now, thanks to you." He doffed his cap and went to stand in the hut.

Still doing his best to appear casual, Raffa packed up the remaining food slowly. Then he spent a few minutes watching some ducks paddle along the riverbank.

Finally he decided that enough time had passed.

He walked toward the little hut, stepped up to the half door, and held his breath as he peered inside.

Slumped in the corner, the fare collector was sound asleep from the combination of califerium and millocham that Raffa had added to the cider.

Raffa was indeed the only passenger on the ferry, and he was glad that neither rower was inclined to conversation at that early hour. He kept his eyes trained on the fare collector's hut. About halfway across, he was rewarded by the sight of a figure emerging from the hut. Raffa had expected the califerium combination to wear off, but even so, he let out a sigh of relief. The man would be groggy for a time, but the infusion would leave him unharmed.

The rest of the crossing was uneventful. Raffa found a spot where he could speak to Echo out of earshot of the rowers.

"Echo, we're going to a big city. A place with a lot of people. While we're there, you mustn't talk to anyone but me. And only when we're alone. Understand?"

"Don't talk," Echo said.

"Except to me."

"Talk Raffa good."

Raffa grinned. "Echo good," he said, and once again found himself cheered by the bat's companionship.

On disembarking at the ferry landing, Raffa walked past a travelers' inn, then up the main road that led north, toward the Commons. It wound through one of the poorest and meanest quarters of Gilden.

Slums rimmed the city to the north and south. The slums had begun as camps for survivors of the Quake, especially those who had arrived in Obsidia from elsewhere; they had become known as the "Afters." Over the generations, some families, like Mohan's ancestors, had been able to move out and establish livelihoods. But many more remained sunk deep in the poverty Raffa saw now.

Spindly-legged children wore soiled rags that could hardly be called clothes. Nearly every home was in a dreadful state of disrepair, fronted by trash piled in malodorous heaps. The smells of filth pressed in from all sides until he could hardly breathe.

Worst of all were the dull and empty gazes of everyone he saw. Whether child or adult, their expressions were those of people who had no room in head or heart for anything but the basest survival. Raffa hadn't known before that hope was the light behind a person's eyes.

But even in such grim surroundings, the day had begun in earnest. Carts and wagons, horses and mules, flocks of ducks and geese, and herds of sheep being taken to market—all were crowded in a chaos of bleats and honks and cursing drivers. Raffa noticed that here on the main thoroughfare no one else was on foot except for those herding the animals. The traffic was too heavy and hazardous.

So he turned off at the first lane he came to, then made a second turning onto another lane that seemed to parallel the main street. But it immediately began twisting, doubling back on itself and leading into blind alleys. It didn't take long before he was thoroughly lost.

He stopped to try to get his bearings. Across the lane, he saw a tiny house that looked a bit better tended than its neighbors. There were no heaps of trash at the doorway, and the window ledge held a few chipped pots of surprisingly healthy herbs and flowers.

Standing at the door was a girl a few inches taller than he was. Most of her blond hair was bound up in a cloth. She balanced a crying baby on one hip. Two more small children sat on the ground at her feet, one plucking at the hem of her skirt, the other playing with her bootlace.

"Shusss, shusss," the girl said to the baby, joggling it gently. She looked up and down the lane. "Where has he got to? I swear I'll topple him—"

She caught sight of Raffa and glared at him, a deep frown-furrow between her eyebrows. "What are you staring at?" she demanded.

"Nothing," he said. "I'm not— I wasn't staring." The confidence that had emerged during his encounter with the fare collector evaporated in an instant. Girls around his own age were always the hardest to talk to.

"In that case, make yourself useful," she said. "You know Jimble? Seen him anywhere?"

Raffa shook his head. "Don't know him," he said. "But could you tell me where the Commons is?"

"The Commons? I'd be headed there myself if Jimble were here! I'll be late, and it's all his fault!" The girl had grown very red in the face and was almost shouting now.

Raffa shuffled a few steps away from her, wishing he had spoken to someone else instead. "Um, if you could just point me in the right direction—"

"And you think you can just waltz in through the gates as if you're a Commoner?"

Raffa was taken aback. He hadn't considered that it might be difficult to enter the Commons, and it occurred to him then that he knew very little about the place. What if he were thwarted in his attempt to reach Garith?

"You're from one of the settlements, aren't you," the girl said with a sniff. "You don't know the least thing about Gilden."

"Not yet, but I will soon enough," he retorted. "I'm going to be living at the Commons. My uncle is already there. He's been appointed a Commons apothecary, and I'm going to be one, too."

He didn't know why he had lied—maybe because he was nettled by the way the girl was scoffing at him.

She narrowed her eyes and looked at him skeptically. "I've heard about the new pothers—there's been talk in the kitchens. They say the Chancellor herself is overseeing them. But you . . . what are you, all of nine years old?"

Raffa bristled. "I'm *twelve*," he said indignantly, "and I've been doing apothecary work my whole life."

But the girl had already lost interest in the conversation and was scanning the street again. Just then a boy darted around the corner and galloped up to them.

"Faults and fissures, where have you been?" the girl scolded. "Wait till I tell Da—"

"Aw, Trixin, don't tell him. I'm here now, aren't I?" Jimble was around ten years old, fair and blond, a smaller male version of his sister. Trixin—so that was her name.

"If I lose my job, where would we be?" Trixin said. "I don't have time to punish you now, but you can be steady sure I won't need reminding later!"

From somewhere distant, a bell tolled once, then again. As the sound faded, it seemed to take all the color in Trixin's face with it.

"Second bell," she said in a voice barely more than a whisper.

Jimble looked fearful. "Quick! Go now and tell them—"

"They won't even let me in after second bell." Trixin's demeanor had completely changed. She had wilted like a broken-stemmed flower.

Raffa felt sorry for her and, in a way, even sorrier for her brother, whose expression was both miserable and terrified. It was clearly Jimble's fault that Trixin would lose her job for not being at work before second bell.

Maybe, Raffa thought, there was a way to help her. And help himself at the same time.

"I have an idea." He spoke much more boldly than he felt. "If you take me to the Commons, you can tell them you're escorting one of the new apothecaries, and that's why you're late. Maybe they'll think that's a good enough excuse."

"You're a pother?" Jimble's eyes lit up with interest. "Can you show me some magic?"

"Jimble, leave off," Trixin snapped. "You're in enough trouble already." Then, to Raffa, "It probably won't work—"

"Course it will!" Jimble burst out. "And besides, what'll you lose by trying?"

Trixin hesitated for a moment longer, then came to life again. She kissed the top of the baby's head and handed him to Jimble. "Beans in the pot for the dinner," she said. "And be sure to keep them all quiet until Da's had his sleep."

She stooped over and untangled her skirt and bootlaces from the fingers of the toddlers clustered at her feet. "Be good and I'll bring you a story," she said to them.

All brisk business now, she started off up the lane. "Come on, then," she said over her shoulder, "you— what did you say your name was?"

"I didn't," Raffa muttered, which drew a giggle from Jimble. "It's Raffa."

As he hurried after Trixin, a much-cheered Jimble shouted after them, "Thanks, Raffa! Come back sometime and show me some pother magic!"

CHAPTER THIRTEEN

"So you work at the Commons?" Raffa said, trotting at Trixin's heels.

"Second assistant, pickles and jams," Trixin replied as she avoided one of the many patches of broken cobbles in the lane.

Raffa pondered her response. There was more than one assistant just for pickles? The Commons suddenly seemed even more intimidating than before. To reassure himself, he reached up and secretly gave the sleeping Echo a gentle pat.

As they came to a crowded junction, Raffa groaned. He could see the Commons in the distance, on a rise overlooking the rest of the city. It would be slow going getting through the traffic—perhaps hours before he reached Garith.

"Don't you know a quicker way?" he asked Trixin.

Trixin narrowed her eyes, staring at him. "Maybe," she said.

Maybe? What did that mean? It had to mean yes, because otherwise she would have said no.

"I have to get to my friend as fast as I can," Raffa said. "And wouldn't it suit you as well, so you can find out about your job sooner rather than later?"

Trixin took a small step closer. "Listen," she said, "I do know a quicker way, but you can't tell anyone. It's— it's a secret."

Anything to reach Garith more quickly. "I can keep a secret," Raffa said.

"All right. . . . See that building there, with the fellow keeping watch?" She pointed her chin toward an inn across the street. A burly man with dark hair and a heavy brow stood in front of the doorway.

"That's an inn for Commoners," Trixin said. "We need to get in there."

Raffa stared at her, uncomprehending. "But neither of us is a Commoner."

Trixin flashed him a look of impatience. "Of course we're not! So we need a way to distract the watchman. What about something from your rucksack? You have all sorts of secret magicals from the Forest, don't you?"

Raffa hesitated for only a moment. He *was* in a hurry to reach Garith. And here was a chance to show Trixin a little of what he knew about botanicals.

A distraction. It would have to be something easy and quick. What did he have with him that might work?

He reached into his rucksack and pulled out something wrapped in a linen rag. "Wait here," he said, and darted up the street.

CRACK! Crack-crack-crack-CRACK!

It sounded like the lash of a half dozen whips all at once. Horses shied and whinnied, there were startled cries from passersby, and two or three babies began to wail. The watchman's head swiveled, and he stared at the street but didn't move from his post.

There was a few moments' silence and then—

Crack-crack-CRACK-CRACK-CRACK!

At this second outburst, a flock of geese being herded to market went into a frenzy of honking and flapping. The geese waddled every which way, snarling the foot traffic. People began shouting and milling about in utter confusion.

And the watchman crossed the street, bellowing for order.

Raffa was alarmed at the furor he had created, but Trixin's eyes were alight with mischief. "I wish Jimble could've seen this!" she said as they scurried toward the now-unguarded door. "What were they? Did you magic them?"

Raffa had scattered a handful of burstbean pods on the street opposite the inn. Unnoticed by the passersby, the pods had exploded harmlessly but noisily whenever anyone stepped on one.

"Not magic," he said. "You can find them in the Forest. I mean, if you know where to look."

"Isn't it dangerous there?"

Raffa couldn't resist the chance to pay her back for her earlier gibe at him for not knowing the city. "Oh, I've been there lots of times. You have to be careful, but it's safe enough if you know what you're doing."

"You couldn't pay me to go there," Trixin said with a shudder.

Raffa cast a glance over his shoulder as they slipped inside the inn, hoping that no one would be hurt in the commotion. First the fare collector and now the inn watchman: He had twice used botanicals for his own ends rather than for healing. Words of reproach sounded in his head—but to his surprise, it wasn't his father's voice he was hearing.

It was his own.

Was it all right to do what he had done, because his goal was to keep Garith from harm? Or was he just making excuses? Raffa squirmed at these uncomfortable questions.

Trixin headed down a short corridor and pushed open a heavy wooden door. Stairs led to a dark cellar crowded with barrels and crates and dimly lit from above by cracks in the ceiling planks. She wove her way between the obstacles. Raffa followed, wondering what they were doing.

There was another door at the back of the cellar. As Trixin held it open for him, Raffa finally had a chance to ask. "I thought we were going to the Commons," he said.

"We are," Trixin said. "There are lots of underground passages like this one. They wander all over the place. But go the right way and you'll end up at the gates. The trick is knowing where to go in and come out. I don't use this way often—only when I'm late. It's faster than the streets."

She stepped through the doorway. "It'll be dark now," she said. "Keep your right hand on the wall to guide you."

"I can do better," Raffa said. He burrowed into his rucksack and pulled out the light stick.

"What is it?" Trixin asked.

Raffa explained. "Go ahead, touch it," he said.

"You sure it won't burn me? Or—or—or turn me into a toad or something?"

Raffa rolled his eyes. *City folk* . . . "If your brother were here, he'd touch it," he teased her.

Trixin made a face, then took a quick poke at the green glow. She immediately examined her fingertip, as if expecting it to fall off. Having survived the ordeal, she looked quite proud of herself.

"Odd upon strange that it's cold," she said. "You'd think there would be some warmth to it."

Raffa handed her the stick. "You're leading, so you take it."

Trixin gingerly took hold of the stick. Then she turned and hurried ahead of him through a series of narrow passageways. From time to time there were a few stone steps, always downward.

In a low voice, she explained why the underground passages were so little-known and used. "Only the guards are supposed to use them," she said. "Most people think they're haunted. But I don't believe that for a second. I think it's just a story made up to keep anyone else from coming down here. The Quake, you know?"

Raffa understood what she meant. So many thousands had been swallowed alive during the Great Quake that for years afterwards rumors had persisted of tapping noises and faint cries for help from below ground. Raffa had been raised to treat such talk as nonsense, but he knew there were those who had never once set foot in the cellars of their own homes—even here in Obsidia, which had been spared the worst Quake damage.

After what felt to him like at least a hundred turns, Trixin paused and whispered over her shoulder, "From here on we have to be really quiet."

Raffa didn't like the sound of that, but she did not explain further.

They continued for a little longer, until the passage ended in a solid rock wall.

Trixin held the light higher. "It looks like a wall, but there are footholds and handholds cut into it," she whispered. "It's a bit tricky—you'll just have to follow the best you can."

"Give me the light," Raffa whispered back. As Trixin began to climb, he put the stick between his teeth. Now he could see what she meant. It was a huge slab of rock with shallow indentations chiseled into its surface. He guessed that it had somehow ended up here as a result of the Quake.

The climb was not an easy one, and Raffa was impressed by Trixin's agility. She seemed to scale the wall as lightly and easily as a squirrel climbing a tree. He followed much more slowly, but the light stick helped reveal the nooks and crannies, and at last he scrambled to the top.

Overhead was a square trapdoor that swung open when Trixin pushed on it. She jumped and caught hold of the edge of the door's frame, then hoisted herself through, one elbow, arm, and leg at a time.

It took Raffa a lot longer to climb through the trapdoor. First he threw his rucksack to her—three times before she caught it. Then he jumped and grabbed the frame. It took all his strength to get his elbows over the edge, and he wondered how she had made it look so easy.

Clearly impatient, Trixin grabbed one of his arms and helped haul him up, at the cost of scraping his stomach against the rough wood.

"Yow," he couldn't help saying.

She turned on him with a fierce glare and put her finger to her lips.

Raffa picked up his rucksack and looked around. They were in another cellar. Unlike the first, this one was empty of all but a few cobwebs. Trixin strode through it quickly, then tiptoed up a flight of stairs to a closed door.

She put her ear to the door and listened for what seemed to Raffa like a long time. Then—

"Get back!" she gasped.

She started down the stairs so suddenly that Raffa was caught off balance. He stumbled backwards, flailing his arms and getting tangled up somehow with Trixin. They fell in a heap at the bottom of the stairs.

Raffa was dazed but unhurt, save for what was sure to be a good-sized bruise on his bottom.

Trixin scrambled to her feet. "Come on!" she said.

Too late. The door at the top of the stairs opened, and a guard in full uniform looked down at them.

"Hoy!" he shouted. "You stay right where you are, the both of you!"

* * *

"Let go of me! I'm telling you, I work at the Commons! Send someone to ask—" Trixin struggled against her captor.

"Shut it!" the guard shouted at her.

Another guard held Raffa tightly by the arm. As painful as it was, the guard's grip was the only thing holding him upright: His legs seemed to have gone boneless.

Arrested for trespassing! Raffa had never in his life been in trouble with the law. His throat burned with fear and shame. How could this have happened? What would Da and Mam say?

He swallowed hard to keep himself from bawling. Trixin, on the other hand, seemed defiant rather than distressed; she continued to screech at the guards. Raffa couldn't help admiring her spirit. At the same time, he was furious with her for getting them into this trouble.

The guards dragged them up the stairs and outside, whereupon Raffa saw that Trixin's secret passage had ended up underneath the guards' barracks. He and Trixin were pushed up against the wall of the building. The two guards stood less than an arm's length away, hands on their bluggen clubs.

"It's the Garrison for the pair of you," one of the guards said.

The Garrison! It was the name of the Commons prison—even the word sounded ominous. Raffa had a pathetic vision of himself huddled in the corner of a dark, dank, rat-infested cell, with no way of getting word to anyone. And instead of heroically rescuing Garith, he himself now needed rescuing. What else could go wrong?

Then he felt a small movement under his tunic. Echo!

His heart pounded. If the guards found Echo, they would surely take him away. Raffa might never be able to find him again!

No. He couldn't let that happen, not in a million years. Raffa felt the strength returning to his limbs. Thinking quickly, he turned around and buried his face in his arm against the wall. He began to make sobbing noises, which in his state of mind was not at all difficult.

"Waah-haah, waah," he cried.

"Oh, foo hoo," said one guard sarcastically.

"Leave off," said the other. "He's just a kiddler."

Raffa never could have imagined that looking younger than his years would be an advantage! But now the guards let him weep away while with his other hand he fished Echo out from under his tunic.

"Don't say a word!" Raffa said loudly between sobs. "Waah, waah! Stay close, and don't talk to anyone, do you understand? Waah-haah!"

His words were directed at Echo, but as he had hoped, both Trixin and the guards thought he was talking to her.

"Quake's sake, who do you think I'll be talking to?" Trixin demanded.

"He's not making any sense," the first guard said.

"*Waaaaaah!*" Raffa cried, still louder.

"Enough of that!" the guard said. He grabbed Raffa by the collar and turned him around to face front again . . . but not before Raffa had seen Echo flutter away unnoticed.

He made a show of snuffling loudly, wiping away tears with his sleeve to cover up the small gleam of hope in his eyes.

CHAPTER FOURTEEN

"WAGON should've been here by now," one of the guards said. "Can't expect us to wait all morning."

Raffa frowned. What wagon? The question was answered moments later when a wagon rolled up, driven by two dour guards in brown uniforms. The solidly built wooden cell at the back had a small barred window in its door. One of the drivers, a woman, jumped down and unbolted the door.

"Got one in there already," she said to the other guards, who then shoved Trixin and Raffa inside. Raffa's rucksack followed a moment later, tossed

unceremoniously into a corner. The door slammed, and
Raffa heard the cruel sound of the bolt being shot home.

The spark of hope he had felt on releasing Echo was
coldly, thoroughly doused. He hadn't even considered
the possibility that they might be taken to the Garrison by wagon! Would the little bat be able to follow it
through the crowded, unfamiliar city?

Once again, Raffa was plunged into wretchedness.
Was there no end to his mistakes and misfortunes? Every
moment of delay was a moment that Garith might be
experimenting dangerously with the vine, and now he
had lost Echo, too.

The wagon started with a lurch. Both Raffa and
Trixin stumbled and fell to the floor. Raffa's shoulder
took the brunt of the fall.

"Oof!" he said. Rubbing his shoulder, he sat up facing
Trixin. "You never said we'd be coming up right under the
guards' barracks!" His voice was loud and angry on purpose; if he shouted, maybe he wouldn't start crying again.

"I've done it lots of times on my own," Trixin
retorted. "If you hadn't made so much noise, they'd
never have heard us. It's all your fault!"

Then she looked past him, and her eyebrows arched
in surprise. Raffa followed her gaze and was startled to

see another girl sitting against the wall.

"A third guest for the Commoners' hospitality," Trixin said.

It was a girl who looked to be about the same age as Raffa. She had deep brown skin, dark eyes, and black hair in neat plaits close to her scalp. And she was studying him closely.

"What are you about?" he demanded. He hadn't meant to be rude, but fear made his voice belligerent and his words curt.

"You look familiar," she said in a gentle voice that made Raffa ashamed of how he'd spoken to her. "I think I've seen you before."

Raffa stared back at her, puzzled. "Where?"

"In the Forest."

"When? I never saw you there."

The girl paused to tilt her head at him. "In the Forest, I don't always feel like talking to people."

Raffa knew exactly what she meant. When he went with his mother on gathering trips, hours might go by during which they never exchanged a word. The sounds of the Forest provided plentiful conversation for them both.

This girl had been close enough there to be able to recognize him here—without him ever seeing her. It was an unsettling thought; at the same time, he couldn't help a twinge of admiration. She was clearly familiar with the Forest and had good woodland skills.

He nodded. "I'm Raffa Santana. I live in the pother settlement."

"Kuma Oriole. From the farmsteads."

"Oriole, like the bird?" Raffa asked.

For reply, the girl whistled an uncanny imitation of an oriole's call. Raffa gave her a tiny smile of appreciation and admiration. Kuma smiled back at him.

Trixin clicked her tongue impatiently. "Just my luck to get stuck with two country lumpkins," she said. "Trixin Marr, second assistant, pickles and jams. Why are you here?"

"I was . . . trying to help a friend," Kuma said. "I pushed a man into the river."

Trixin hooted, then looked at Kuma with new respect. "That sounds like a story!" she said.

"I'm sure it's a good one," Raffa said, "but not for now."

"Why not?" Trixin scowled. "It'll take at least half an hour to get to the Garrison, maybe longer. A good story will pass the time."

"We have other things to talk about."

"Oh, we do, do we? Who made you a senior, baby-face?"

Any other time, Raffa would have seethed over that epithet, and he did in fact feel a little rankled. But the need to reach Garith and to find Echo were far more important, and he decided to ignore Trixin's remark.

"We have to figure out how to escape," he said.

"Escape!" Trixin threw up her hands. "It's even worse than I thought. Don't they teach you how to count out there in lumpkin-land?" She began ticking off on her fingers. "Two guards here in the wagon. One in the Garrison's gatehouse. Two up top at the door to the cages, two down below—"

Cages? Raffa shivered at the word, then resolutely shook off the shivers. "Wait," he said. "How do you know so much about the place?"

"My business, not yours," she snapped.

Were all city dwellers so prickly? "Look," Raffa said, "I'm trying to help someone, too. And it's urgent. So if there's even a tiny chance for me to get out of here, I have to try."

Even if he did manage to escape from the wagon, Raffa knew that he'd most likely end up back at the Garrison; there was no way he could outrun all of Gilden's guards.

But he needed to evade them only long enough to get to Garith. He'd warn Garith about the vine and tell him to search for Echo. It was far from a perfect solution, but it was the best he could come up with.

Kuma nodded. "I'll go with you," she said, "and help however I can. But Trixin is right. I don't know anything about Gilden."

Trixin glanced between Kuma and Raffa. Finally she tossed her head. "Quake's sake! Then I'll have to help as well. If I don't, the two of you are sure to get caught before you even leave the wagon!"

She looked up at the ceiling for a long moment before continuing. "My da was in the cages. For three months last year. He was man-of-all-work for a senior—a misery of a master, paid next to nothing. Cook let Da go through the scrap bucket, the one that was kept for the dogs. He brought the best scraps home to us."

Her eyes glittered with anger. "The cook didn't mind. She said the senior's dogs were all too fat and lazy, anyway. But one day the senior saw him. Cook got in trouble, too, but he likes her food, so she kept her job. But my da was arrested."

She choked out a mirthless laugh. "Can you imagine— arrested for stealing from a *dog*? Of course, he could get no decent work after that, and now he's a night slopper."

Night sloppers. Although there were none in the pother settlement, Raffa had heard of them. They walked the streets of Gilden after dark, collecting the buckets of human waste left outside the homes of the wealthy. The waste was poured into large vats that were wheeled to the outskirts of the city. Then the sloppers mixed the waste with straw and leaves so it could be dried for compost.

There was no lowlier job in the land.

Now Trixin lifted her chin. "That's why I know the Garrison. I came to see him here, twice. Then he told me not to come anymore, he was that ashamed."

"But it wasn't his fault!" Kuma exclaimed.

Trixin gave her a grateful look. Then her eyes went steely and she spoke crisply. "Right, so I figure our best chance is as soon as they open the wagon door. Once we're taken through to the cages, we won't have a prayer."

Raffa scooted to the corner where his rucksack lay. "I can't believe they didn't take this away from me," he said. One of the guards had searched the sack for weapons, finding nothing but what Raffa had heard him call "some seeds and twigs."

"They wouldn't dare," Trixin said. "The Garrison's warden would have their heads. Prisoners' belongings go to him for safekeeping"—her voice took on a sarcastic edge—"never to be seen again."

Raffa arranged his apothecary jars and bundles on the floor of the cell. He did a quick accounting of each substance's uses, which served as both a reminder to himself and a brief lesson for the girls.

By the time the wagon creaked to a stop, they had managed to patch together a plan. The odds that the three of them could outwit the Garrison's guards were terrible. Aside from being strong and well-trained, the guards would have both armor and weapons: javelancers, bluggens, and chuckers, according to Trixin.

Raffa and his cohorts had nothing but surprise—and botanicals.

The door opened, and the guard peered into the dim interior.

"Wha's this, then?" she said.

Trixin lay on the floor. Her eyes were closed. She was curled on her side with her head toward the door and her hands behind her back. Raffa and Kuma sat on opposite sides of the wagon, leaning against the walls.

Both looked frightened, and Raffa knew that on his part it wasn't an act.

"She hit her head," he said.

"Can't she walk, then?" the guard demanded.

"Ask her yourself," Raffa said.

"Watch your tongue," the guard snapped. "Wake up, girl!"

She shook Trixin's shoulder roughly. Her head lolled back, but otherwise she didn't move.

The guard turned and spoke over her shoulder. "Have to carry this one in," she said. "Go get someone to help."

The other guard's footsteps faded into the distance. It was better than they'd hoped: Now there was only the one guard left.

The guard barked, "You two stay right where you are." She climbed in through the door and took hold of Trixin under her arms, preparing to drag her.

With the guard leaning directly over her, Trixin sat up so fast that her forehead caught the woman squarely on the chin. She cursed in pain as Trixin rolled to one side.

Kuma was on the move, too. She held a cloth packet containing a small amount of rust-colored powder.

She threw the powder into the guard's face. The guard roared, clapped her hands to her eyes, and dropped to her knees.

It was cappisum powder, made from dried red peppers. Raffa had explained to the girls that it was used for poultice combinations to relieve headaches and other pains. But in its pure powdered state, it caused terrible searing and burning of the eyes.

The guard was blocking the doorway, but Trixin took care of that by shoving her shoulder. Still screaming in agony, the guard fell onto her side. Then the three prisoners scrambled over her and out the door.

They leapt from the wagon, Raffa following Trixin, with Kuma right behind him. The guard in the wagon was shouting curses at the top of her lungs, and a colleague at the gate came running. This one was wielding a javelancer.

Forcing himself not to look at the weapon, Raffa ran straight toward the guard. Then he stopped in his tracks and looked up to see a sneer on the man's face.

"Makin' this too easy," the guard snarled.

It took every bit of Raffa's nerve not to run as the guard advanced. *Wait,* he shouted to himself silently. *Wait . . . wait . . . NOW!*

Raffa's arm swung out. From a jar in his hand, he pitched a silvery liquid to the ground in front of the guard's feet. The guard took one more step, tripped, and fell with a deafening clatter of armor. His feet had gotten stuck in the silver puddle, a combination that included sap from an irongum tree, the stickiest substance known to apothecaries. When he hit the ground, one of his knees and an elbow also stuck fast.

"What in the name of the Quake?" he roared.

There was no way he would be able to pull himself free. He'd have to take off whatever garments and armor were stuck to the sap, which should delay him considerably.

As the guard continued to shout in anger and indignation, Raffa accidentally touched the rim of the jar. To his chagrin, the jar stuck firmly to his hand.

Kuma and Trixin were running toward the gate. Raffa galloped madly after them. He could see the street now. It seemed much brighter and more colorful than the Garrison's grim courtyard.

And it looked close. So close . . .

"Hurry!" Trixin urged over her shoulder.

She was first to the gate. Raffa saw her grab the bars and pull—

"NO!" she cried out.

The gate was locked.

Raffa ground his teeth. How could they not have thought of this? Trixin was still jerking at the gate, which rattled but didn't budge.

"What do we do now?" Raffa asked.

"Do I have to think of everything?" Trixin shouted back.

Raffa thought this a little unfair, considering that both the cappisum powder and the irongum sap had been his ideas. "The key," he said.

"Brilliant," Trixin said, her voice sharp with sarcasm. "Do you suppose they'd give it to us if we asked nicely?"

"At least I'm trying to think of something!" Raffa shouted back.

He looked back at the irongummed guard, who had given up trying to get himself unstuck and was now screaming for help. How long before reinforcements arrived?

Then Kuma hissed at him and held up a big iron key.

"How—?" he gasped.

Kuma pointed at the gatehouse just inside the entrance, where he could see an empty hook on the wall.

While he and Trixin had been arguing, Kuma had simply walked over and taken it, so quietly that he hadn't even noticed.

"Hurry!" Trixin said. "They're coming!"

Raffa saw two more guards running from the door to the cages. Kuma inserted the key into the lock, but it refused to turn. In desperation, Trixin shouldered Kuma out of the way and jiggled the key, to no avail.

Raffa and Kuma shrank back against the gate, with Trixin beside them. Seeing that the prisoners were trapped, the guards slowed their pace as they approached.

"Nothin' but three little kittens," the tall guard sneered.

"Kittens like rats, don't they?" his stout colleague responded. "Plenty of rats where they're going."

The tall guard reached for Kuma. Just then something wet and viscous fell onto his forehead and dripped into his eye.

"Hoy—what's this?" he exclaimed, and tried to wipe away the mess.

The stout one began laughing. "Splootch!" he said. "Yer covered in bat splootch!"

Bat splootch?

His pulse jumping, Raffa searched wildly overhead.

A moment later, the stout guard made a gagging noise. A large blob of guano had landed in his beard and mustache.

"Where is it?" the tall guard shouted.

"Aarghableah!" the stout guard choked out, wiping his mouth in disgust.

Both turned their faces skyward. Trixin slipped behind Raffa and began fiddling with the key again.

Then Raffa felt a soft *whump* as Echo missed his perch and landed with his claws in the tunic.

"Ouch!" Echo squeaked.

"There—on the boy!" yelled the stout guard. He pointed his bluggen club menacingly at Echo.

Raffa reacted without thinking: He swung his hand through the air and brought the jar crashing down on the bluggen. The jar broke in half, and the rest of the irongum combination splashed about. The guard instinctively jerked his bluggen upward in defense—and the sticky end touched his beard.

"Faults and fissures!" The guard's face purpled with anger. He jerked hard to free the bluggen, then bellowed in pain as part of his beard ripped off.

At that moment, there was a dull clank, followed by a shrill metallic squeal. Trixin had finally managed to

turn the heavy key in the rusted lock and was now tug-
ging on the gate. Every head—whether prisoner, guard,
or bat—spun to look at her.

Raffa and Kuma made to run, but it was too late.
They were within reach of the guards, each of whom
made a grab for one of them. Raffa cried out as his arm
was jerked hard by the tall guard.

Echo managed to disentangle his claws from the wool
and launched himself directly into the tall guard's face.
The man yelled and dropped Raffa's arm as he waved
the bat away.

Echo began circling around the guards' heads, flapping his wings madly. "Raffa good!" he squealed. There
was no mistaking the degree of his indignation.

The guards were so astonished that Raffa almost
wanted to laugh—and Trixin *did* laugh, despite looking
just as surprised.

The guards glanced at one another uncertainly. "Did
you hear—" the stout one started to say.

"You hear, you hear!" Echo echoed shrilly.

The tall guard backed away. "It's magic!" he said in
alarm. "Forest magic, it has to be!"

His partner looked at him uncertainly. In that moment
of the guards' hesitation, Kuma plucked at Raffa's sleeve

and tugged him toward the opening. As Echo continued flapping around the guards' heads, with an occasional deafening high-pitched squeal thrown in for good measure, the three prisoners became escapees—and ran for their lives.

CHAPTER FIFTEEN

RAFFA stumbled on the cobblestones and staggered into pedestrians. He kept trying to run, but there were too many obstacles on the crowded streets. At one point he risked a look over his shoulder to check for guards and, to his joy, saw Echo careening toward him. He slowed down and held out his arm. Echo slammed into his sleeve. "Ouch!"

Raffa wondered if Echo was finally using the word correctly. But he had no time to examine the bat. Hastily he tucked the perch necklace under his tunic, then started running again.

He grew dizzy from trying to keep Trixin and Kuma

in sight while looking over his shoulder every other moment. Panting hard, he had to stop to let a cart pass. As he waited anxiously, he heard a shout behind him.

"HOY! You boy—stop!"

The guards had spotted him. His heart jumped and he dodged around the cart, nearly getting his foot caught under one of its wheels. Then he looked up and discovered to his horror that he could no longer see either Kuma or Trixin. He'd never get away on his own. Not here, not in the city . . .

He felt the blood draining from his face. In a panic, he turned off the street into a narrow lane. It was even more crowded than the street, with people and dogs and buildings so close together he could hardly breathe.

Then his arm was grabbed from behind. With a strangled gasp, he whirled around, striking out with his free hand.

"Raffa, stop! It's me, Kuma!"

He could hardly see or hear anything through the confusion in his brain. When his vision cleared, he saw Kuma's face, and the tension left his body so quickly that he almost fell.

She caught his arm. "This way," she said, and led him through the doorway of what appeared to be an abandoned building. They went down a set of rickety wooden stairs into a dark, low-ceilinged cellar.

More by feel than by sight, they groped their way to a far corner. Trixin was already there, hiding behind some discarded crates and broken barrels. For several moments they sat in silence, all three of them listening hard. The street noise seemed far away, and Raffa heard no thump of guard boots. At last, they looked at each other in wary relief.

Under Raffa's tunic, Echo gave a little squeak. Raffa pulled out the necklace. Both girls gasped.

"That bat *talked*," Trixin said. "I couldn't believe it. I still can't believe it—but I know what I heard! How in the world—"

"It's a long story," Raffa said. "But the short of it is, I'm not even exactly sure why or how he can talk."

"Why or how, why or how," Echo said.

Trixin made a huffing sound. "Oh, I see now. He's not really speaking—he's just echoing you."

Raffa was about to reply indignantly when Echo stretched his wings and fluttered to hang from a beam overhead.

"Dark good," the bat said. "Cave human?"

"Er, never mind," Trixin said.

Raffa grinned. "We're in a cellar, Echo. Underneath a house, and, yes, I guess you could say it's like a cave for humans."

Then he sobered. "I didn't want anyone to know," he said. "If people find out, something bad might happen to him. Someone might try to kidnap him."

Kuma made a small noise of distress but said nothing.

Raffa looked at the girls pleadingly. "You can't tell anyone. You have to swear you won't!"

Trixin looked momentarily disappointed. "Can't I tell Jimble?" she said. "And the little ones? It would be such a good story for them!"

Panic rose in Raffa. "No! They'd never be able to keep a secret. Please, Trixin, you have to promise!"

"Steady on," Trixin said. "If it's that important to you, I won't tell."

"Swear it," Raffa demanded.

"Fine—I swear! But you have to promise to tell me the whole story sometime."

"I swear, too," Kuma said. "And he's lovely, but . . ."

Her dark eyes wide and soft, she leaned toward Raffa. In a voice as firm as it was quiet, she said, "Animals aren't meant to talk."

Raffa stared at her in surprise. Was there a right and

a wrong about Echo's ability to speak? He had been so excited at first, and then so delighted with the bat's companionship, that he hadn't considered the question before. He wondered how Echo himself felt about it and decided to ask the bat when they were alone again.

Trixin spoke briskly. "Enough about the bat," she said. "We need to talk about something really important: How are we going to get into the Commons?"

"I thought we agreed," Raffa said, "that you'd say you were escorting me, and—"

"That won't work anymore," Trixin said. "They'll send word from the Garrison about the escape, and all the gatekeepers will be watching for us—for two girls and a boy. We'll be back in a prison wagon quicker than a clap."

Raffa had to bite the inside of his cheek to keep from crying out in frustration. It was already almost sunpeak, half the day gone, and he wasn't any closer to speaking to Garith than when he got off the ferry.

"We need a different plan," Trixin said. "What else is in that rucksack?"

Raffa shook his head. Using the cappisum powder and the sap combination had indeed helped them escape—but in another sense, it was a giant stride in the wrong direction. Earlier, he had used botanicals for purposes other than healing; now he had actually used them to hurt people.

The cappisum powder would wash off. The other guard's patch of beard would grow back. There would be no permanent damage. But Raffa had been lucky, and he knew in his very core that he had gone against the principles of apothecary ingrained in him since birth.

"I don't know what else I could do," he said slowly. Which was true enough. He certainly wasn't accustomed to inventing such uses for botanicals.

"What if we were all disguised somehow?" Kuma asked.

Trixin eyed her curiously. "Don't tell me you need to get into the Commons, too?"

She nodded. "My friend—the one who's in trouble—I think she might be there somewhere."

Kuma's suggestion of disguises set Raffa to thinking. If Trixin and the Garrison guards were typical of city dwellers, then besides being frightened of the Forest, many of them thought of apothecaries as magicians. Perhaps this was something that could be used to their advantage. . . . An idea shaped itself in his mind.

"A new apothecary will be arriving at the Commons

shortly, right?" he said. "So let's get to work on that."

Both girls had plenty of notions for improving Raffa's plan, resulting in some heated discussion and several changes of mind as they worked. When at last they had finished their preparations, they examined each other using Raffa's light stick. And in spite of their anxious uncertainty, all three of them had to stifle a spattering of giggles.

A long line of people waited at the east gate, hoping for permission to enter the Commons. From the rear came a ripple of surprised movement as the crowd made way for a small procession.

Walking abreast, an arm's width apart, were two creatures who could have been gnomers or throlls from an ancient story. They were barely taller than children, and one was terribly humpbacked. They crouched and sidled low to the ground, like crabs. Eyes circled in green and lips dead white, each held their hands cupped before them, bearing a mysterious corked jar.

Raffa was the humpback, wearing his rucksack stuffed under his tunic. He also wore a complicated turban (Trixin's headscarf) pinned in place with a brooch that looked extraordinarily like an enormous real beetle.

It *was* a real beetle, one of the supply he had brought with him to feed Echo. Kuma had unplaited her hair, which now stood out like a dandelion puff and was seeded with red and gold berries (from Raffa's jars).

Trixin followed them. Her hair was piled high, which made her look taller. She had stripes on her face in half a dozen colors. Lips coal black, and eyes peering out from vivid starbursts of red, she held her head proudly and stared straight ahead, at the gate.

Raffa took a deep breath and bellowed in what he hoped was a throll-like voice. "Clear the way! Clear the way for the Great Trixarina, apothecary from the deepest heart of the Forest of Wonders!"

The queuers gasped as one and fell back.

"The Great Trixarina" stopped several paces short of the gatehouse. Raffa crabbed his way up to its half door, where the gatekeeper was stationed.

"Senior Gatekeeper, I attend the Great Trixarina!" he said. He was so nervous that his voice was shaking, so he spoke even louder, trying to drown out the tremors. "No ordinary apothecary is she! From the dark heart of the Forest of Wonders, sh-she honors Gilden with a once-in-a-lifetime visit!"

The gatekeeper gawped for a moment, then snapped

into officiousness. He made a show of examining the slate on the wall of the gatehouse.

"Not on the list," he said. "No Trixa—hem, no Trix-alixer on the list."

Kuma in her puff-haired gnomer guise stepped forward and began a singsong chant. "The list, what list? It's wrong, it's wrong! The list is wrong! What list? All wrong!"

The gatekeeper huffed and sputtered, his indignation making it apparent that it was he himself who had made the list. At that moment, a runner raced up to the gatehouse.

"Urgent word from the Garrison, Senior!" She handed the gatekeeper a strip of blond wood on which a message was chalked.

Raffa froze. Just as Trixin had predicted, the Garrison was sending round news of their escape. Despite the hump and the turban and the thick layers of color on his face, he felt naked with fear. They would be caught now, and sent back to the Garrison. He would never reach Garith in time. He would languish in that rat-filled cell for weeks, maybe months. . . .

Kuma began a mad dance, whirling, kicking, and leaping about like a deranged toad, all while yodeling nonsense at the top of her lungs. She danced her way over to Raffa, then grabbed his arm and almost yanked it out of its socket.

"YOW!" he shouted.

Kuma spun him around and pulled him toward her. "Dance," she whispered, glaring at him.

Suddenly he understood what she wanted. "Yow-wow-wow!" he screeched as he too began dancing. They bounded about in front of the gatekeeper, gibbering and gabbling. Then they started popping up and down, thrusting their corked jars into the man's face.

"We come from the Forest!"

"The Forest of Wonders!"

"The Great Trixarina!"

"Trixarina the Great!"

The gatekeeper cringed but then managed to gather himself. "Enough!" he roared. "Shakes and tremors, has the Forest made you all ziggy?"

He looked down at the strip of wood, then handed it back to the runner, who sprinted away with it to the next stop on her rounds. Raffa and Kuma exchanged quick glances. Would the gatekeeper see through their disguises?

Trixarina took a step forward. The hum and buzz of the crowd faded as people strained to hear her speak.

"Senior Gatekeeper," she said. Her black lips parted in a ghastly smile, but the crowd behind her couldn't see that. "In the regrettable absence of my name from the list, it seems that you have a choice. You can send word to inquire of the Chancellor, for it is she who oversees the new Commons apothecaries."

"Th-th-the Chancellor," stammered the gatekeeper.

"Yes. But of course you knew that. However, if you would prefer, I could give you a demonstration of my skills as proof of my claim to entry."

Trixarina's voice remained pleasant, but her two attendants raised their jars high over their heads. They leered and cackled madly.

"A nice big blue wart on your forehead? Porcupine quills instead of hair? Or perhaps"—Trixarina put a finger to the side of her nose thoughtfully—"tusks. Yes, I think a pair of tusks would be most handsome. And I daresay you might find them useful in your profession." She held out her hand toward gnomer Kuma, who loped over and proffered the jar.

The gatekeeper's eyes had grown larger with each suggestion and were now wide with alarm. It was clear that all thought of the message from the Garrison had left his mind.

"Oh, well now, that's all right, Missum—er, Triskadooda," he said in a fluster. "Won't be necessary, wouldn't dream of troubling you. Come right on through, you and your . . . er . . . your associates."

Throll Raffa and gnomer Kuma waltzed through the gate and into the Commons, followed by the Great Trixarina.

CHAPTER SIXTEEN

RAFFA wanted to skip and leap and crow in triumph. The disguises had worked—they'd made it past the gatekeeper! Best of all, no one had gotten hurt.

But the charade continued, for they still had to reach the apothecary quarter. While planning the scheme, Trixin had said that once they were inside the gate, any Commoners who saw them would think they were part of a performing troupe. She was right: The trio drew a few curious glances, but otherwise no unwanted attention.

The Commons spread out over a vast expanse, with no building higher than a single story. A network of covered walkways connected the buildings. Nearly every structure was made of wood. Long ago, it was discovered that wooden buildings had withstood the Quake better than any other kind, so ever since, all of Obsidia's architecture was built of wood.

Except, of course, for the glasshouse. When it came into view, Raffa gasped in amazement. He had never seen so much glass in one place! From a distance, it looked like a vast emerald, glinting and gleaming in the sun. How marvelous it must be inside! Maybe he could take a look now, just a quick one. . . .

No—how could he even think such a thing? The glasshouse was of no importance at the moment. What if he was too late to warn Garith about the scarlet vine—what terrible affliction might he already be suffering from? With a shudder, Raffa recalled the dreadful cracks on his hand, which seemed to tingle with the memory.

Trixin directed them around the back of the glasshouse to a building at least three times the size of Raffa's home. It was newly built; he could smell freshly cut wood. They were now out of sight of the main walkways, so Raffa and Kuma straightened out of their crouches with twin sighs of relief.

"We did it!" Kuma said, a huge smile lighting her face.

"I nearly popped laughing when you started that—that dance or whatever you were doing!" Trixin exclaimed. She held out her hands toward Kuma, who clapped them in celebration.

"What a panic!" Kuma said. "I thought I'd have to break Raffa's arm to get him to do something—anything!—when that runner showed up!"

"Did you see the gatekeeper's face when I threatened to give him tusks?"

Raffa did not join the celebratory chatter; he was too anxious to see Garith. He trotted to the door of the building, lifted the knocker, and rapped three times; his heartbeat pounding in his ears sounded nearly as loud.

Almost immediately, he heard footfalls within, and the door opened.

It was Garith. And he looked to be in the prime of health!

Raffa stood on the doorstep, overcome at the thought of finally reaching his destination after everything he had been through. He didn't know whether to laugh or cry, to hug his cousin or punch him.

Garith seemed equally overcome. What else would explain his utterly puzzled expression?

"Er, hem . . . can I help you?" he said.

Raffa opened his mouth, but no words came out. He saw Garith glance past him; his eyes widened and he made a sound that was half cough, half laugh. Raffa turned to see that Trixin and Kuma were now behind him—still in their bizarre disguises.

"Oh!" Raffa said, rapping his own noggin. "Garith, it's me, Raffa!"

"*Raffa?*"

"Yes, yes, I know I look ridiculous, but it's really me—" He spit on his hand and rubbed off some of the green around his eyes. "See?"

"But—but why are you dressed like that?"

"Garith?" From somewhere inside the building, Raffa heard his uncle's voice calling. "Garith, who is it?"

Ansel emerged from a door at the rear of the entry hall. He looked, if anything, even more puzzled than Garith had been. "Who are these people?" he demanded of no one in particular.

"Da, it's Raffa!" Garith exclaimed.

"*Raffa?*" Ansel said in astonishment. "But how— Why did you not send word that you were coming? Where are your parents? And what in the name of the Quake are you wearing?"

Raffa had never in his life felt so relieved. He started

to laugh, then laughed harder, and couldn't seem to stop. His uncle and cousin stared at him in bewilderment.

"Nephew, are you all right?" Ansel asked in a concerned voice.

Finally Raffa's laughter faded out with a few last giggles. "Yes, Uncle, I'm fine," he said, gasping for breath. "These are my friends, Trixin and Kuma. May we come in?"

While Ansel led the girls toward the back of the building, Garith took Raffa through a door off the entry into a small room that held a narrow bed and a chair.

"You can leave whatever you want in here," Garith said. "I'll fetch you some wash water." He looked Raffa over again and shook his head, still obviously bemused.

"Yes, but I need to talk to you first." Raffa inhaled, wondering if his pulse would ever return to normal. Then he spoke in a rush. "I know you took a clipping, and it's okay—I should have given you one, anyway. But Da and I have been working with it, and, Garith, it's really powerful. You have to take care upon caution—I came all the way here to tell you so. That's how dangerous it is."

There was a beat of awkward silence. "I meant to

tell you that I was taking one," Garith said. "Sorry I forgot. And Da's been— you should ask him about the clipping. He'll be able to— well, anyway, I'll get that water now." He left the room quickly.

Garith's response seemed more than a little odd, but Raffa put it aside while he checked on Echo. The little bat was apparently exhausted by his brief but fierce burst of activity at the Garrison, during what for him was a choice time for sleep. Now he hung from the perch looking so deep in slumber that Raffa could even imagine him dreaming. Of midges, probably.

Raffa found himself regretting that Trixin and Kuma had heard Echo speak. Could he really trust them not to tell anyone? And what of the guards at the Garrison—would they soon spread the word throughout the Commons? It might be too late, but he was still determined to do whatever he could to protect Echo. He vowed to keep the bat's speaking ability a secret from everyone else.

He struggled out of his rucksack. Then he undid the turban and shook his hair free, wondering if it was his imagination or if Garith had really been uncomfortable talking about the vine.

But when his cousin came back with a pitcher and a

basin, his usual easy enthusiasm had returned. "Hurry up now, so I can show you the laboratory. Wait till you see it. It's better than good!"

Raffa felt a rush of relief and gladness. He had no idea what would happen next, but for the moment he decided to enjoy the fact that Garith was fine and that they were together again.

Scrubbing the green paste of herbs from his face was like washing away all the worry and fear and dread of the past several hours. The white substance on his lips, a combination of allbus berries and milk root, was unfortunately rather more stubborn; he hoped the traces that remained in the creases of his mouth would wear off soon.

"This way," Garith said.

They crossed the entry hall, and Garith pushed open a door into a fairyland.

Raffa stared in wonder. A broad counter ran around three sides of the spacious room, with cupboards and open shelves above and below. There was a huge worktable in the middle of the room. In the far corner stood a large iron stove; flanking the stove were twin stone basins.

At the center of one long wall was an enormous

cabinet with dozens of small drawers perfect for storing botanica. Everything an apothecary would ever need was well organized and easily at hand: mortars and pestles, spoons, strainers, scales; tongs and tweezers; beakers and jars and tubes and vials; funnels and siphons. Without taking a single step closer, Raffa could tell that each implement and device was the finest of its kind. His fingers itched to be working with such beautiful tools.

In a sudden flood of emotion, he realized that this was where Ansel and Garith were now working every day. The same would be true for him if it weren't for his father's stubbornness! Standing there in the doorway to the laboratory, he made himself a silent promise: He would work here. And not just someday, but *soon*.

"Raffa?"

Uncle Ansel's voice broke into his thoughts. Raffa blinked and saw that his uncle was seated at one end of the table with Kuma and Trixin, who were both now disguise-free. There was a plate of bread and cheese as well as a bowl of apples and pears, and Trixin was pouring tea.

Raffa realized that he was famished, having eaten nothing since breakfast with the fare collector so long ago, on the other side of the river. He sat down next to

Kuma and eyed the food hungrily.

Ansel smiled kindly. "Why don't you all have something to eat first, and then we can talk."

The three visitors fell on the food, with Garith keeping them company. In very short order, every last bite had been swallowed. Raffa sighed and took a long draft of his tea.

"Now, then, Raffa," Uncle Ansel said. "Please tell us how you and your friends come to be here."

Raffa glanced up warily. He had not discussed with Trixin and Kuma what they would do or say at this point; their entire focus had been first on escaping from the Garrison and then on gaining entrance to the Commons. But Ansel and Garith were family. He could not possibly keep the truth from them.

He stared into his mug for a long moment. Then he looked at his uncle and began to speak.

"I crossed over on the dawn ferry," he said. Then he talked for what seemed like a very long time. He told them about losing his way on the streets of Gilden and running into Trixin. About getting caught at the guards' barracks, meeting Kuma in the prison wagon, and escaping from the Garrison. About disguising themselves by painting their faces with botanicals.

Raffa didn't mention every last detail. He left out how he had used apothecary on the fare collector and the guards. He said only that he and Trixin had been caught trespassing at the barracks, not how they had gotten there. And he said nothing at all about Echo's presence and role.

"We managed to get past the gatekeeper," he said, "and—well, now here we are."

For the entirety of his story, he had looked only at Ansel, encouraged by the fondness and keen interest on his uncle's face. Now he surveyed the others. Garith was twirling an apple core by its stem, looking not so much bored as restless. Raffa guessed that Trixin was thinking about the loss of her job, because the frown-furrow between her eyebrows had returned.

But it was Kuma who startled him. Her whole face was suffused with despair, and he wondered what could possibly be making her so sad.

"Well, nephew," Ansel said soberly. "That was quite a trip, and taken on the whole, it seems we are fortunate that you arrived safely. The first thing is to send word to your parents that you are here. I will arrange for that."

"Thank you, Uncle," Raffa said. He realized then that he had been squelching the guilt he felt toward his parents, and he hoped that the message would reach them quickly.

But what then? Would they ask his uncle to bring him home? Or might they come to Gilden to fetch him? He sat up a little straighter at this last thought. If his parents saw the apothecary quarter for themselves . . . maybe there was a chance they would want to stay and work here!

"Uncle," he said, hesitant and eager at the same time, "would you . . . could the message invite them for a visit? And they could take me home after that?"

He did some quick guesswork. Once his parents knew he was safe, they would in all likelihood remain at home long enough for Salima to attend the birth of the young mother she had been looking after. That would give him at least a few days here.

Ansel smiled. "That's a splendid idea, Raffa." Then he sobered. "But there is a more serious problem to be discussed. You and your friends are now fugitives who have escaped from the Garrison. The guards will be searching for you."

The air in the room grew thick with silence. Raffa squirmed, realizing only then his uncle's difficult position. Ansel was at the moment sheltering escapees from the Garrison, which was surely a crime. And it was Raffa's fault.

Garith spoke up. "Da, the Chancellor. Maybe she could help."

"The Chancellor!" Trixin exclaimed. "Why would she help someone like me?"

"Not you, exactly," Garith said, "but she likes us a lot. Especially me."

Raffa had to chuckle inwardly. He could tell that Garith wasn't bragging; he was simply telling the truth.

And Uncle Ansel chuckled aloud. "True enough that she seems to have taken to you. It is our best chance. I will go to the chancellery and ask to speak to her."

Then Trixin spoke up quickly, as if she were afraid her courage would fail her. "Senior Vale, Raffa wanted me to help him find his way to the Commons, and because of everything that happened, I . . . well, obviously, I'm not at my post in the kitchens today, and I'm sure that by now I've been discharged. Please, I know this is too bold of me, but my family—they depend on me working. Is there any chance . . . could you ask about me getting my job back?"

Ansel looked sympathetic. "I'm afraid I would have no influence in such matters," he said. "But I will see if anything can be done."

Then he turned his attention to Kuma. "What about you, Kuma? Raffa said he met you in the prison wagon. Why were you there?"

Raffa was sitting next to Kuma, and he sensed her body tensing as she spoke. "I was—a friend of mine was in trouble, and I was trying to help her," she said. "I pushed a man into the river. I didn't mean to, but he grabbed me to stop me from getting to her, and I shoved him away and he tripped."

Ansel seemed astonished. "Remarkable!" he exclaimed. "I received word this morning of just such an occurrence. How extraordinary that you were involved." For a long moment, he studied Kuma intently. Then—

"Kuma, the friend you were trying to help. Is she, by any chance, a very large bear?"

CHAPTER SEVENTEEN

RAFFA gasped. A bear? The girl who had tamed a Forest bear—*that was Kuma?*

It was Garith who found his voice first. "I can't believe it! Is it really tame? How did you do it?"

"No," Kuma said. "She's not tame. She's a wild bear. The Forest is her home."

Ansel looked at Kuma, his eyes bright with admiration. "We heard the rumors," he said, "but I never dreamed they could be true. What an amazing thing you've done."

Kuma bowed her head at the compliment and seemed to relax a bit.

"Please tell us more," Ansel said.

She was silent for a moment. "I was only four years old," she began slowly. She went on to tell of a family outing to a meadow near the Forest. She had strayed away from the group and gotten lost. It had started to rain, and despite a frantic search, no one heard her cries as she wandered about for hours, wet, cold, alone, frightened.

"Then this huge bear came out," Kuma said. "From the trees. I was too little to know any different. I just ran straight toward her."

"Faults and fissures!" Trixin exclaimed.

"I don't remember very much more," Kuma admitted. "But she must have taken care of me. They found me days later, in the same meadow. My family could hardly believe I'd survived all those nights alone."

She paused, then went on. "Except I wasn't alone. As soon as I was old enough, I started going to the Forest to try to find her. And I finally did, when I was seven." Another pause. "Or maybe it was she who found me. She made this lovely noise, 'A-rooo, a-rooo,' so I called her Roo. Ever since then we've spent . . . a lot of time together."

"Amazing," Uncle Ansel repeated.

"Such a story!" Trixin said.

"But where is she now?" Kuma's voice quavered. "They took her from the Forest in a wagon. To the Commons, I heard them saying." She looked at Ansel. "Please, will you help me find her?"

Raffa saw tears in Kuma's eyes. He knew then that this bear meant even more to her than Echo did to him. His fear that Echo might be taken from him—Kuma was living that very nightmare with the bear, and his heart ached for her.

Ansel's hesitation was so brief that Raffa thought he might have imagined it. "I know only that a bear was captured, nothing more. I will find out what I can."

"Thank you," Kuma whispered.

"Has anyone sent word to your family? I should have asked earlier."

She shook her head. "No, it's all right. They know—I mean, I'm often away from home, so they won't be worried."

That sounded odd to Raffa, and apparently to Ansel as well. "Are you sure?" he asked.

"I'm sure," she said. "I live with my aunt and uncle, but I stay in the Forest a lot. They'll think I'm there now."

After a pause, she added, "They have six children of

their own. They're not unkind but . . . it's just easier for everyone when I'm not around." She squared her shoulders and looked at each of them in turn, as if daring them to pity her.

Raffa felt a flash of . . . perhaps not pity, but regret for Kuma, followed by a ripple of gratitude for his own family.

"All the same, they need to know where you are," Ansel said. "I'll add a note to send along with the one for Raffa's parents." He pushed his chair back and stood. "I will go now to the Chancellor. Garith, please take our guests to the apartment so they can get some rest. I will meet you there later."

Raffa jumped to his feet and clasped both of his uncle's hands. "Thank you, Uncle," he murmured. "I'm so glad you're here."

After Ansel left, Garith led the others to the apartments where he and his father lived. It was only a short walk from the apothecary quarter.

The apartments were built around a central courtyard. The Vales' residence was on the west side. The door from the courtyard led into an entry hall, with a simply furnished but spacious sitting room on the left.

Off the sitting room was a separate kitchen. "And this is the pantry," Garith said. "You can eat whatever's there. And over here . . ." He showed them to the other side of the entry hall. "Not just sleeping alcoves—real bedrooms!" Three of them, one each for Garith and Ansel and a third for guests.

"So much space for just the two of you!" Trixin's eyes were wide. Raffa remembered Trixin's tiny home, smaller than the sitting room alone.

"Raffa, you rest in here in my room," Garith said. "Wait till you get in the bed. It's feathers, not straw, you never slept on anything so comfortable in all your life!"

Thanks to the featherbed and sheer exhaustion, Raffa fell asleep almost the instant he lay down. He woke an hour or so later. It was nearly sunfall.

He got up, put on his boots, and went out to the sitting room. Uncle Ansel had returned; he and Garith were sitting with Kuma and Trixin in front of the hearth.

"We were just going to wake you," Ansel said with a broad smile. "I have very good news!"

He had seen the Chancellor, who had fixed everything. Well, almost everything. For a start, she had arranged for Raffa and Trixin to be pardoned, both for trespassing and for their escape.

Raffa gave a whoop of joy and relief, and clapped his hands around Garith's in celebration. "But what about Kuma?" he asked, glancing at her solemn face.

"Kuma, the charge against you is assault," Ansel said, "and a penalty had to be assessed for such a serious charge. But I'm happy to report that you will spend no time in the Garrison. You have been assigned to serve the Commons for one month. It is the most lenient sentence possible, and the Chancellor has asked me to supervise your service."

Kuma nodded. "Senior Vale, did you . . . Is there any news about Roo?"

Ansel shook his head. "I'm sorry, no. But the Chancellor promised to make inquiries."

Kuma looked down at her hands, and again Raffa could tell how much she missed the bear.

Ansel turned to Trixin. "Trixin, your position in the kitchens—"

"Second assistant, pickles and jams," Trixin broke in.

"Yes. I'm afraid that a replacement has already been hired."

Trixin went pale, and her lower lip quivered a little. She cleared her throat. "I—I understand," she said. "But whoever it is, it's hard to fathom that they need the job as much as I do."

Ansel held up his hand. "Pickles and jams," he said. "So you understand fermentation?"

Trixin looked puzzled by the question but answered eagerly. "Oh, yes, Senior, both brine and vinegar. I can pickle anything—I could pickle an old shoe if you wanted me to!"

Now Ansel smiled. "It so happens," he said, "that two days ago I put in a request at the staffing depot for an assistant to work with us here in the apothecary quarter. I specified a hireling with experience in fermentation."

Raffa knew that some botanicals were fermented before being used in combinations. It was a tricky process, for the line between fermented and spoiled was all too easily crossed.

Trixin's eyes grew round with surprise. "You mean—?"

"Before you accept," Ansel said, "you should know that unlike your previous post, this is not a servient position. It is tendant level, with greater responsibility and"—he paused to let his eyes twinkle at Trixin—"better pay."

Amazement followed by delight shone from Trixin's face. "I— Oh, thank you, Senior Vale!" she said, and bowed over her fists. "I swear to you, you'll never have reason to regret this!"

She rose from her seat. "I should be getting on for home," she said, sounding reluctant.

"Your new job starts tomorrow," Ansel said, which made her smile broadly as she said her farewells.

Raffa stretched his legs in the warmth of the fire, feeling better than he had in days. If only Kuma and the bear could be reunited, all would be well.

"And now a surprise," Ansel said. "The Chancellor has invited us to dine with her tonight. We should leave promptly."

"Solid-earth!" Garith cheered. "We've dined there before. The food's always better than good."

Dinner with the Chancellor! Raffa could never have imagined such an honor. "Do I—are my clothes all right?" he asked, looking down at his tunic.

"You're not to worry," Ansel reassured him. "It's not a formal gathering, only ourselves."

"Senior Vale?" Kuma's voice was as quiet as Garith's had been loud. "I don't mean to be impolite, but I'm feeling a little unwell. If it's not too discourteous, would it be all right if—if I stayed here to rest?"

"Of course," Ansel said. "I will give your apologies

to the Chancellor. Would you like a tonic?"

"No, thank you," Kuma said. "I'm sure I just need more rest."

Before leaving for dinner, Raffa managed a few moments alone with Echo, who had begun to stir under his tunic. He decided not to take the bat with him. Although he hated the thought of being separated from Echo again, it wasn't fair to keep him cooped up for so long, especially as it was his feeding time.

Raffa cracked open a shutter in Garith's bedroom. He hung his rucksack on a nearby peg and hid the perch necklace behind it.

"Echo," he said in a low voice, "this window opens onto the courtyard, see? You can go hunting. But don't leave the courtyard. When you're done, come back inside to your perch. And remember, don't talk!"

Echo gazed at him with his purple eyes wide but made no reply.

Raffa frowned. "Do you understand, Echo?"

"Don't . . . talk." Echo's whisper was barely audible, and Raffa grinned as he released the bat into the dusk.

CHAPTER EIGHTEEN

WITH Kuma comfortable in the guest bedroom, the rest of the group set out for the Chancellor's residence across the Commons. As they were shown in by a tendant, Raffa tried to look everywhere at once.

The Chancellor's quarters were elegant but not ostentatious. For Raffa, the greatest marvels were the oil lamps ensconced on the walls: They had glass chimneys and burned with a brightness and clarity that rivaled daylight.

Chancellor Leeds stood in the doorway to the dining room. She was a tall woman of striking looks. Her skin was smooth and tan, and she had green eyes and silver hair like a cloud around her head. Solidly built, with a regal bearing, she wore a simple cream-colored tunic and matching trousers. In her presence, Raffa suddenly felt like—what was it Trixin had called him?—a country lumpkin.

The Chancellor greeted them warmly. Then Garith said, "Are we eating soon? I'm all hollow!" Seeing how easy Garith was with her, Raffa decided to try and relax, too.

She led the way to the dining room. Before they were seated, Ansel explained Kuma's absence, and the Chancellor called for one of the fine place settings to be removed. She directed them to their seats, Ansel at her side across from the boys.

"If you would please remain completely silent for the next few moments," she said, her eyes bright with a secret smile. "No matter what happens."

Then she raised her pointer finger high in the air. "Beak, deliver!"

Four chickadees flitted in from a doorway across the room. In their beaks they held silver balls the size of small plums, which they dropped onto the brass serving charger in front of each diner.

The balls landed with a barely audible thud, and Raffa saw that they were made of a shiny, tissue-thin fabric, crushed and wadded into shape. Before he could even draw a breath, one of the chickadees landed on the edge of his charger. With its little beak, it began pecking at the fabric ball.

Raffa sat transfixed by what the chickadee was doing. Only at the last moment did he notice that something seemed a bit different about the bird. What was it, exactly? Before he could examine it more closely, it gave a triumphant chirp and flew off with the others.

The bird had opened the fabric ball into a square—a napkin! Raffa looked up to see his surprise reflected in the delight on the faces of the other three. The Chancellor smiled and nodded but gestured for continued silence, then raised her finger again.

"Ink, deliver!"

This time, four crows flew in. They, too, alit on the edges of the chargers. Each crow placed something triangular on the napkin. It was made of pastry and gave off a tantalizing buttery, savory smell.

Garith could no longer contain himself. "They're mine! The crows are mine!" he almost shouted. "Why didn't you tell me?"

His outburst startled the crows: Some flapped, others squawked, and the one on Raffa's plate did both, then tumbled off its perch. As it righted itself, Raffa's mouth fell open in astonishment.

The crow's eyes were purple.

Like Echo's! But what did it mean? Purple eyes, the same as Echo's . . . It couldn't be just a coincidence.

Then he realized that Echo's eyes *had* been black before. Their color had changed after Raffa treated him; it was the scarlet vine that had caused the transformation. If Garith was treating these birds, their purple eyes could mean only one thing: He was already using the vine!

But why hadn't he told Raffa when they talked about the vine earlier? *Ask Da,* he'd said. . . . And with all the excitement, Raffa had completely forgotten to talk to Uncle Ansel about it.

Then another thunderclap of a thought shook him: Could the crows talk?

All this occurred to Raffa in a mere blink of time; meanwhile, the Chancellor was responding to Garith. "I wanted it to be a surprise," she said, smiling broadly, "to show your father and cousin the results of your fine work."

"There's more to be done," Ansel said. "They still get distracted by loud noises."

"Yes, but it was a steady good show!" Garith said proudly.

If indeed the crows had the power of speech, wouldn't that have been part of the demonstration? Certainly, Garith would have wanted to boast of it. Raffa's best guess was that Echo's ability remained unique. But what that meant about the scarlet vine's properties and effects was still a mystery—one that he was determined to solve.

The Chancellor raised her finger in the air again. "Ink, away!" she said.

Everyone watched as the crows rose into the air and flapped out of the room.

"Now, Senior Vale . . . As we discussed?"

Ansel cleared his throat importantly. "Raffa," he said. "The Chancellor is doing you a great honor. We have been hard at work on a special secret project, and I have convinced her that you should be told about it."

A secret project? Raffa's eyes widened. He glanced at the Chancellor, who was looking straight at him. "I confess that on meeting you just now, I was surprised," she said. "You seem . . . rather young."

Raffa sat up as tall as he could. "I'm less than a year

younger than Garith," he said, trying hard to keep his voice respectful.

"And when it comes to apothecary, you would think him the elder," Ansel said, smiling.

Garith scowled. The Chancellor saw his sour expression. "That would make him talented indeed," she said. "Young Vale has done fine work here."

Her words seemed to placate Garith, whose face relaxed. "Chancellor, it's true," he said with a generous wave of his hand. "Raffa is quite good at apothecary."

"I am glad to hear it," she replied. "I do hope he'll be able to make a valuable contribution to our project. Please go on, Senior Vale."

Every hair on Raffa's head bristled with indignation. Garith, patronizing him like that! And the Chancellor, doubting his abilities, talking about him as if he weren't there! At least Uncle Ansel believed in him and was now looking at him earnestly.

"As you may have guessed, nephew, the project has to do with the training of animals," Ansel said. "It has been under way for several months now, and while the trainers have achieved some degree of success, progress has been slow and arduous."

"We decided to hire apothecaries," the Chancellor

said, "to develop infusions that will make the animals easier to train. And it's already working. After Senior Vale developed a new infusion, the crows achieved more in a few days than in the entire month previous."

The vine . . . already being used in such a new way! Raffa almost bounced in his chair with excitement. This was what he had been hoping for! Uncle Ansel's daring attitude meant progress in bold strides, not stutters and shuffles.

"The birds you saw tonight are only the beginning," the Chancellor continued. "Imagine the possibilities. Not just pretty tricks but real work. If we succeed as we have envisioned, we can free people for more noble employment, while animals take over the most odious and drudging of tasks."

What an astonishing idea! Raffa had never imagined apothecary being put to such a use. "But why is it a secret?" he asked.

The Chancellor's expression grew sober. "We fully expect to succeed at our endeavor," she said. "But there are still problems to be worked out. I'm sure you can understand that we do not wish to announce the project publicly until we are assured of its flawless execution."

That made sense. Responsible apothecaries never

announced new treatments until at least a dozen trials proved them sound, so Raffa could understand and respect the Chancellor's desire for prudence.

"Now, I know you must have many more questions," the Chancellor said, "but it has already been a long day. Vale, I trust you will show him everything he needs to know."

"It will be my pleasure," Ansel replied.

The Chancellor raised her arms and spread them wide as if including them all in an invisible circle. "Welcome, young Santana," she said. "Welcome to our project."

Raffa bowed his head over his joined fists, the traditional gesture of great respect.

All through the rest of the meal and then on the walk back to the Vales' apartment, Raffa's mind was hum upon buzz. Now more than ever, he was determined to become one of the Commons apothecaries, so he could work with the vine in that wonderful laboratory, and then experiment still further.

He would make new discoveries, and find his own path as an apothecary, not the one worn down by his father.

For the moment, he put aside the problem of how to

convince his parents to move to the Commons. Before their arrival—in a few days at most—he had to impress the Chancellor. He needed to come up with something that would prove how useful he could be to the project.

Raffa was so preoccupied with this problem that he barely said good night to his uncle. Sharing Garith's bed—much bigger than those at home, so they didn't have to sleep head to toe—he fell asleep still pondering.

The next morning, a loud crash woke him. His heart leapt as he sat straight up to see Garith standing by the bed, grinning.

"Oopah," he said, "I kicked that stool over, didn't I. Come on, sleepydeep, I've been waiting ages for you to get up!"

Raffa began to carp at his cousin but stopped in mid-grumble, now wide awake. The noise of the stool, the way his heart had jumped . . . He knew what to do now and could hardly dress fast enough to start the day.

"Keep your voices down," Uncle Ansel said as the boys shouldered each other through the kitchen door-way. "That Kuma certainly loves her sleep!"

After a quick breakfast, they walked to the labora-tory. Raffa turned his idea over in his head. It might not be possible. Certainly he had never heard of anything like it being done before . . . but then, wasn't that the point? If he was serious about wanting to do new things with botanicals, he would have to get used to doubt and uncertainty.

And if it worked, no one would ever again think of him as "too young." Not the Chancellor, not his father. He lifted his chin as he walked, his jaw set.

Trixin was waiting for them at the laboratory door, early and eager for her first day at her new job. "Steady morning to you all!" she called out.

"And to you, Trixin," Ansel said with a smile. "Here is a list of ingredients and equipment needed from the kitchens. I'd like you to fetch them, then arrange a space in the laboratory as a fermentation area."

"Yes, Senior!" Trixin looked as if there were nothing in the world she would rather do, which was probably true, and Raffa smiled as he watched her depart, list in hand.

Ansel turned to the boys. "I have a meeting with Senior Jayney," he said. "Garith, I want you to show Raffa around and then make a new batch of the training infusion. As for Raffa—what task shall we set you?"

"Uncle, I'd like to make an infusion for the birds," Raffa said.

"What kind of infusion?" Garith asked, sounding a little defensive.

"They get startled by loud noises, right?" Raffa said. "I want to work on something that might help with that."

"Excellent!" Ansel said. "If you should succeed, it would be a great step forward for the project. I'll return before midday to hear how things are going." He left them with a cheery wave.

Raffa could hardly believe the change in his fortunes since the grim desperation of the previous day. This morning, life in Gilden was unfolding exactly as he had dreamed: he and Garith given free rein to work unsupervised in the beautiful laboratory!

Garith began by taking Raffa into the glasshouse. The air was warm and gently humid; it felt *green* inside his lungs. It was quiet, too, but Raffa was filled with the sensation of hundreds of plants busily growing.

He marveled at how cleverly the space had been arranged. In addition to tables and shelves filled with plants, there were also cantilevered tiers overhead. They were staggered to ensure that all the plants received ample sun, and rigged to pulleys so they could be easily reached. Every available bit of space was being used.

Garith lowered one of the tiered shelves. Raffa gaped:

On it were at least three dozen clippings of the scarlet vine, each in its own small jar.

"How did you get so much of it?" he exclaimed.

Garith shrugged. "I don't know," he said. "I showed the vine to Da, and a few days later, these were here. We made a distillation from querco chips. They're not growing very fast, but they're doing a bit better than when they were in plain water."

Raffa felt a flash of admiration and a twinge of annoyance at the same time. He should have thought of that himself.

He reached for one of the clippings, and Garith took another. Back in the laboratory, Raffa set his jar on the counter and stared at it. What sort of combination might temper a crow's hearing?

He searched his memory. A year or so earlier, Missum Rezon from the settlement had sought out Salima. She had complained of dizziness, and Salima had treated her with an infusion of willow bark and zinjal and sent her home with a week's supply. Missum Rezon had returned a few days later: The dizziness was gone, but she could no longer hear in her left ear. Salima instructed her to stop taking the infusion. The ear cleared, and the dizziness did not return.

Perhaps, then, a highly diluted solution of the combination, with the scarlet vine added, would have the desired result? Raffa went to the cabinet and took a moment to run his eyes over the neatly labeled drawers. He had never seen so many botanicals in one place.

He took powdered willow bark and zinjal from their drawers, combined them, and added water to make a solution, which he put to boil in a glass beaker. Then he began to grind a short length of the scarlet vine.

At the other end of the worktable, Garith was doing the same with his clipping. "What happened with the vine—you know, back home?" he asked.

Raffa told him about the frightening cracks on his hand. Garith nodded. "We had a garble with it here, too," he said, "starting with what you told me you used on the bat—the combination for strengthening, with the vine added. Shakes and tremors, what a disaster!"

"Why, what happened?"

"We gave the infusion to a squirrel and—ah, it's almost impossible to describe!" Garith said with a shudder. "It started *screeching*. Sure upon certain, I've never heard such a dreadful noise in all my life. It felt like our bones were being shredded! I blacked out, and Da almost did, too."

"How did you get it to stop?" Raffa asked, horrified.

"Sheer luck. I'd been holding it down, but I let it go to cover my ears—which didn't work, the sound penetrated everything—and the thing started running around like a maniac. After I blacked out, it ran straight into the door and stunned itself."

"Faults and fissures!" Raffa exclaimed. "The poor thing—was it hurt badly?"

"I don't know. . . . I don't think so," Garith said. "Mannum Trubb came and took it away. He's Senior Jayney's assistant. They're in charge of training the animals."

At the mention of the injured squirrel, Raffa realized, aghast, that he had completely forgotten about Echo! He'd been so preoccupied trying to think of something that would impress the Chancellor . . . but how could he have neglected the bat?

He forced himself to think calmly. Even if Echo had stayed out all night hunting, as he often did at home, he would have returned to sleep away the daylight hours. He was now surely right where he belonged, in Garith's room, on the perch hanging behind the rucksack. Raffa would check on him as soon as he finished working on the new infusion.

He went back to pounding the vine. "What are you making now?" he asked.

"The training infusion," Garith answered. "Before we got here, the trainers were using califerium and millocham"—Raffa recognized the standard combination for sedation, which he himself had used on the fare collector—"to make the birds and animals easier to train. But they were having a lot of trouble with the dosage. Either too sleepy or too crabby."

Garith continued grinding the vine in his mortar. "So then I told my da how well the vine had healed the bat, and he decided to try adding it to the combination. I had to make at least ten different batches, using all different quantities, but we finally got it right. It makes them calm but not dopey."

Raffa couldn't help thinking about the large quantity of the vine Garith must have used before he found the right proportions. He looked up to see Garith staring at him.

"I know what you're thinking," Garith said with a scowl. "You'd have done it twice as fast. No, five times as fast. Go on—tell me I'm wrong."

"At least five times," Raffa said lightly, trying to make a joke of it.

But Garith didn't seem to find that answer the least

bit funny. "Well, I'll have you know, the Chancellor herself came to the laboratory specially to thank me."

Raffa wondered why his cousin sounded so resentful, but he didn't want to ask. For a while they worked in silence. Using a marvelous set of tiny spoons, he began adding the pulverized vine to the solution. As he did so, he sensed vibrations in his mind.

Two vibrations. Two different frequencies. With the smallest spoon, he measured in minuscule amounts of the vine pulp. Slowly, the vibrations grew more coordinated. It was a tranquil, easy feeling, as if time itself had calmed and slowed.

He realized how much more relaxed he felt, working without Mohan over his shoulder. Surely it wasn't wrong to heed his instincts at such moments. His father was right in that he shouldn't depend on intuition alone, but couldn't he learn to let it be a guide, not a tyrant?

One more tiny spoonful: The vibrations in his mind melded together perfectly. The infusion turned from olive green to a transparent scarlet, then began to glow and sparkle.

He stared at the glass beaker in wonder: It looked as if it were filled with rubies. Or at least what he imagined rubies looked like, having never actually seen any.

Garith glanced over at the beautiful infusion. Then, to Raffa's astonishment, he slammed his pestle on the tabletop in disgust.

"It's so easy for you!" he cried out. "All the pothering stuff—it always has been!"

"Garith, I—"

"No, you don't understand! You've never understood! This is the first chance I've ever had to—to do things without you around making me look bad! And now that you're here, you'll just show me up all over again. Da will say nothing but 'Raffa this,' 'Raffa that.' I'll never hear anything else!"

He shoved away his mortar and stomped out of the room, leaving Raffa wide-eyed and openmouthed, the spoon in his hand forgotten.

Garith didn't want him here. Raffa grunted as that knowledge took hold, not in pain but as if his insides were being emptied out. His first thought was to leave Gilden: He wouldn't stay where he wasn't wanted.

But then the emptiness filled with indignation, which in turn became belligerence. It wasn't up to Garith whether he stayed or not! He had just as much right to be working here as Garith did. His family had been invited, too!

He didn't know what to do. Should he go after his cousin? Leave him alone? Ignore the outburst, or try to talk about it?

No, Garith clearly didn't want Raffa anywhere near him. He turned back to the table and began cleaning up, thinking of one of his mother's favorite sayings. "Work helps keep worry at bay."

She was right, too; he was able to push the unpleasantness with Garith to the back of his mind as he concentrated on figuring out how to dose a bird.

Now all he needed was a crow.

CHAPTER NINETEEN

A S Raffa finished his preparations, the door opened and Ansel entered. He was followed by Garith—and the Chancellor. Surprised, Raffa bowed over his joined hands.

"Steady morning, young Santana," the Chancellor said. "Senior Vale has informed me of your experiment. I hope you don't mind my presence here."

"N-n-no, of course not," Raffa stammered in reply.

In truth, he was dismayed to have an audience, especially one that included the Chancellor. He would much have preferred to test the infusion privately. But there was no help for it now, and he tried to reassure himself that it would be good for the Chancellor to see firsthand the extent of his skills.

Garith had a crow perched on his arm and was busy stroking its feathers. He did not look at Raffa, but Raffa couldn't tell if it was deliberate avoidance or not.

"Nephew, this is one of the trained crows," Ansel said. "For testing your infusion. Are you ready?"

Raffa nodded. He measured a spoonful of the ruby-hued solution into a saucer, then took a crust of bread and crumbled it into the liquid. He waited a moment before tilting the saucer to make sure that all of the liquid had been absorbed by the bread. It was the best way he could think of to get the bird to take the infusion.

"I've been using a dropper," Garith said loudly. "It's worked fine."

He set the crow down on the tabletop. It promptly spotted the saucer in front of Raffa and let out an interested "Cra-a-aw."

It was a handsome bird, its glossy feathers so black that in places they gleamed blue. Like all of its breed, it didn't hop as other birds did: It walked across the table, looking almost human.

Then it cocked its head to look at the saucer. Raffa saw its purple eyes, which immediately reminded him of Echo.

Echo, who was no longer just a bat, but a friend and companion.

In that moment, Raffa felt a wrongness from somewhere deep in his bones. Just as the crow stretched out its beak for a piece of the bread, he snatched up the saucer and held it away from the bird.

He couldn't do it.

A healer, Mohan had called him. A healer would never use an infusion designed to cause harm. And if the infusion worked, that was exactly what it would do: It would make the bird hard of hearing, take away one of its basic faculties. Garble enough to cause such an affliction by accident, but to do it intentionally was yet another step on the road away from the true intent of apothecary.

"What are you doing?" Garith said, as the crow squawked angrily and beat its wings in frustration.

Unable to meet the eyes of anyone else in the room, Raffa looked from the bird to the saucer and back again. This was supposed to be his big opportunity to impress the Chancellor! She was standing not five paces away, along with Uncle Ansel, who had vouched for him. And Garith, who was already angry at him.

What would they think? Could he make them understand?

He made a quick decision rooted in desperation. "It's not ready," he said. "I just remembered that I—I left out one of the ingredients."

Ansel stared at him, the skepticism in his eyes bordering on disbelief.

Raffa could almost hear his thoughts: *Shakes and tremors, you haven't forgotten an ingredient for a combination since you were five years old!*

Garith snorted, then coughed to cover it. Was it Raffa's imagination, or did he seem pleased by the failure?

The Chancellor shifted restlessly. "Add it, then. My schedule is as always a busy one. I cannot spare much more time here."

Raffa forced himself to speak even as he shrank from her words. "I'm afraid I can't do that. I have to start over, with a new batch of solution." He dared a quick peek at her expression. Her eyes were hooded in disappointment.

"That's our Raffa," Uncle Ansel said heartily in an obvious attempt to lighten the air in the room. "Such a perfectionist! I tell you, Chancellor, it is this kind of conscientiousness that makes for a good apothecary."

Raffa wanted to hug his uncle right then and there. He could only hope that the Chancellor would see things in the same light.

She was silent for a moment, and Raffa feared the worst. Would she forbid him further work here? Or send him home?

"I'll leave it with you, Senior Vale," she said at last. "You know the boy and the project. If you think he will be of some assistance, he may continue to work, at least until his parents arrive. You will, of course, ensure that he does not delay our progress."

Raffa felt his face grow warm with embarrassment and anger. He had to remind himself that he had done the right thing and that Uncle Ansel had at least gained him some more time.

The Chancellor departed, and Ansel suggested tactfully that they return to the apartment for lunch. "Garith, Raffa and I will go on ahead. Will you see to things here?" He made a vague gesture with his hand. "You can put the crow in its cage. Mannum Trubb will fetch it later. Come, Raffa."

Raffa understood that his uncle meant to speak with him alone. As they walked back to the apartment, Ansel put an arm around Raffa's shoulders.

"Nephew," he said, his voice kind, "why don't you tell me what really happened back there?"

Raffa was not about to heap another lie on top of

the one he had already told. And it was just him and his uncle now; it seemed easier to tell the truth without Garith and the Chancellor there.

"I couldn't do it, Uncle," he said. "It's not right, using apothecary to take away their hearing."

Ansel's expression grew thoughtful. "When it comes to our art, Raffa, you are always ahead of your years," he said. "Let me ask you, do you also think it wrong that we are using the sedative infusion to make the animals easier to train?"

Raffa considered the question for several moments. Then he asked, "With the scarlet vine added, does it still wear off?"

Ansel nodded. "Yes. We have to dose them for each training session."

Raffa spoke slowly. "Then I think it's okay. As long as the trainers are kind to them . . . That infusion— it's temporary, it isn't meant to harm them. It's different from one that would damage their hearing. Especially when we don't know whether it would be permanent."

Ansel nodded. "Apothecaries who dare to experiment often face difficult decisions," he said.

Raffa said nothing. A troublesome thought had come to him. He believed everything he had said to Uncle

Ansel, but was it also possible that he had lost his nerve? That he wasn't brave enough to face the uncertainty of experimentation?

"Raffa, this project is of enormous importance," Ansel continued. "The Chancellor believes it will change life here in Obsidia for the better. My interest goes beyond that—I want to extend the reach of apothecary art. I see this project as only the beginning."

They had reached the apartment, and as they entered the courtyard, Ansel had a final word for him. "The infusion is your creation, Raffa. Think on what we have discussed. We will keep it safely stored, and you alone will decide what to do with it."

Raffa couldn't speak for a moment, so great was his gratitude for his uncle's understanding. Ansel had spoken to him almost as if he were an adult—as an apothecary, a colleague. "Thank you, Uncle," he said solemnly. "And I will think on it, I promise."

But he already knew that he could never use the infusion to deafen an animal. He would have to find some other way to prove himself to the Chancellor.

Once inside, Raffa hurried into Garith's bedroom. He took his rucksack off the wall peg—and gaped in unhappy shock at the vacant perch.

He rushed to the window. It was still ajar; Echo should have been able to enter easily. Frantically he scanned the room—was the bat hanging from the ceiling or the walls?

No Echo.

Raffa stuck his head out the window; the bat wasn't outside under the eaves. His throat tightened as he imagined the worst: Echo, kidnapped by someone who had discovered he could talk. They would put him in a cage, take him traveling "for profit," just as his mother had warned, and Raffa would never see him again. . . .

He ran back into the main room, searching the walls and the furnishings. Ansel was putting a trencher on the table.

"What's the matter, Raffa?"

Raffa banged on the door of the room where Kuma was staying. "Kuma!" he said in a low, urgent voice. "Wake up! Have you seen Echo?"

Ansel came into the hall and pushed open the door.

The bed was neatly made. Kuma wasn't there.

Raffa felt like tearing his hair out. Garith angry at him, Echo missing, and now Kuma gone too!

Ansel frowned. "I should have made it clear to her that she was not to go anywhere without my permission.

Does she not understand what it means to be sentenced?"

"I'm sure she's gone to search for the bear," Raffa said. "She seemed really worried about it."

He ran back into Garith's room to grab the perch and his rucksack, then helped Ansel gather up some food for lunch. They hurried back to the laboratory.

"She's my responsibility for the term of her service," Ansel muttered, speaking more to himself than to Raffa. "She'd better show up soon, and with a very good explanation."

Preoccupied as he was, he didn't notice Raffa anxiously scanning the sky and the buildings and every tree they passed. When they arrived at the laboratory, they found that Garith had tidied up after Raffa's failed experiment and was busy unpacking the goods Trixin had brought from the kitchens.

"Where's Trixin?" Ansel asked.

"Fetching a few more things," Garith said. "She should be back any moment now."

"Have something to eat quickly," Ansel said, and explained about Kuma.

They ate where they stood, and even though Raffa's mind was rife with worries, he sensed the tension in the air between himself and Garith. As if he weren't feeling bad enough already . . .

He had never given serious consideration to how his own gift might affect his cousin. Garith's words echoed in his head. *You'll just show me up all over again.* Raffa recalled the tightness in his voice, so unlike his usual easy manner. Garith, good at everything . . . except the one thing that mattered most to his father.

Raffa was jerked out of his thoughts by a loud thumping at the door.

"Garith! It's me, Trixin. Hurry!"

Garith threw open the door, and Trixin almost fell across the threshold. Breathless, her headscarf askew, she was holding a box about the size of a loaf of bread, covered with a cloth.

"An emergency," she panted. "A servient stopped me—from Senior Jayney—he gave me this, and told me to hurry—to be careful but hurry, so I didn't run, but I walked really fast."

She set the box down on the countertop. With Raffa and Garith crowded around her, she lifted the cloth and cried out, "Oh, the poor things!"

Garith drew in a hard hiss of a breath through his teeth.

Raffa stared at the contents of the box, too shocked to make a sound.

Two baby raccoons lay curled on their sides, one at each end of the box. Their fur was caked and matted with blood; Raffa could not even see where they were injured. Their eyes were open, staring at nothing. They looked dead—but then Raffa saw the slightest movement of breathing in both their chests.

"He—the servient—he said that Senior Jayney needs you to try to heal them. Oh, but look at them. They're hurt so badly!"

Ansel took a quick look in the box. "Ears, everyone," he said. "Raffa and Garith, you will treat these raccoons. Trixin, you'll assist them. I will search for Kuma, and if I cannot find her, I'll have to alert the guards to keep an eye out for her. I'll be back as soon as I can."

"Kuma's missing?" Trixin said, and Garith explained quickly.

Ansel hurried off. Garith waited until the door had closed behind his father, then spoke to Raffa. "You treat one, and I'll treat the other," he said with what seemed to be a trace of wariness. "You take the lead. Whatever you do, I'll do exactly the same."

Was this Garith's way of making up? Or was it sheer practicality, considering how often his own apothecaria came out amiss?

Raffa had no time to ponder further. With a final, fervent wish for Echo's safety, he put aside his concern for the bat and turned his full attention to the injured little animals in front of him. He picked up one of them gently and put it into another box, which he handed to Garith.

Trixin hurried to stoke the fire in the stove and put on a kettle of water.

The first thing Raffa did was clean his raccoon's fur. The wounds were horrifying. Three terrible lacerations striped the animal's back, with two more on its head and neck. One ear was badly torn, and there was a deep ragged puncture on the left haunch. The little raccoon made a single feeble attempt to rouse itself and nip at Raffa's hand, but it fell back immediately.

As had happened when he first saw Echo, the urgent desire to help a suffering creature surged through Raffa. It was an odd feeling—not purely sympathy but sympathy combined with the fascination of a challenge. Could he do it again? Could he heal such terrible injuries and return the raccoon to a worthwhile life?

And even as he knew it was a selfish thought, he realized that the raccoons were providing him with another, unexpected chance to prove his worth as an apothecary.

"The vine," he said to Garith tersely. "We'll need more of it. Enough to make both a poultice and an infusion."

Garith took Trixin to the glasshouse and returned with two clippings. The boys set about preparing the same poultice that Raffa had used on Echo.

Raffa turned the pestle, and his paste began to quicken.

"Oh, look!" Trixin exclaimed. "How lovely!"

Garith glanced up and saw the scarlet sparkles in Raffa's mortar. His face instantly closed in disappointment: His paste showed not a single trace of gleam or glimmer. Raffa felt torn between pity and a flash of ignoble pride. But more than either, he wanted to be on good terms with his cousin again.

"Trixin, will you bring me another clipping, please?" Raffa said. He gave his mortar to Garith. "Use this," he said. "I'll make some more."

Garith's expression was both sullen and pleading. "Don't tell Da," he muttered.

"Tell him what?" Raffa said, expressionless, and hoped he was not imagining the small sense of warmth from Garith.

He made a second batch of poultice and applied it to

his raccoon's wounds. Then Trixin and Garith bound the wounds of both raccoons while Raffa began work on the infusion. He found the combination for the strengthening tonic in the cabinet, made a solution, and added the vine pulp.

"Mine's female," Garith said, bent over one raccoon. "What's yours?"

"Male," Raffa replied. "They must be twins. They look to be the same age."

Garith showed Raffa how to use a dropper to dose the raccoons. The dropper was a clever device consisting of a hollow tube capped with a bulb made of rubber— yet another marvel of the laboratory. Garith squeezed the bulb, then released it to draw the infusion into the tube. While Raffa held the raccoon's little jaws open, Garith placed the end of the tube far back in its mouth, then squeezed the bulb again. The infusion went right down the raccoon's throat.

"That was easy," Raffa said in admiration. "Way better than using a reed."

Garith nodded; they repeated the routine for the second raccoon. Trixin made two soft beds of rags for the little beasts, and their boxes were put side by side on a shelf above the stove to help keep them warm. There was nothing more to do but wait until the raccoons regained consciousness.

Then Raffa was shaken by a sudden apprehension: *What if the raccoons can speak when they wake?* Surely Uncle Ansel or Garith would add two and two to make four and wonder about Echo, who had been given the exact same infusion.

Uncle Ansel knew him too well. He'd known that Raffa was lying about the treatment for the crow; there was no way he could expect to get away with another lie about Echo. Once his uncle found out, he might feel compelled to tell the Chancellor. A talking bat—such a wonder . . .

What would she do? Would she order Echo taken away from Raffa, to become part of the project?

He gulped down his panic and forced himself to think methodically. He had to find out if the raccoons could speak before anyone else did, which meant being alone with them when they first woke.

And he had to find Echo.

CHAPTER TWENTY

"GARITH," Raffa said, his voice urgent. "Echo, the bat . . . I brought him with me to Gilden. But he's gone missing, and I have to find him."

"I didn't know he was with you," Garith said. "Why didn't you tell me before?"

"It's been really busy ever since I got here," Raffa said. Which was true enough. In his mind he added, *And you've been so angry at me that we've hardly spoken all day.* "I want to check the apartment, in case he's there now."

"We shouldn't leave the raccoons alone," Garith

said. "They're too badly injured. I'll stay here to watch over them."

"Then I'll go with Raffa," Trixin said. "I've seen the bat before, I know what he looks like, and I know the Commons."

Raffa scurried to the door and held it open, shooing Trixin out before she could say anything about having also *heard* Echo before.

They began walking quickly. "I haven't told them yet—about Echo talking," Raffa said. "I still don't want people to know."

"Not even your uncle?"

"If I don't find Echo today, I'll tell him," Raffa said. He wasn't really answering Trixin's question because he wasn't sure of the answer himself. It would be awful if he had to put Uncle Ansel in the uncomfortable position of keeping the secret from the Chancellor—and worse still if his uncle wouldn't or couldn't.

Raffa recalled Kuma's quiet words: *Animals aren't meant to talk.* Much as he hated the idea, it was starting to look as if she might be right.

"First that bat and now the raccoons," Trixin said, shaking her head. "And here I thought this job would be about plants, not animals! Those poor little raccoons. They're so young. I wonder what happened to their mother."

On impulse, Raffa asked, "What happened to yours?" Then he bit his tongue. Maybe she wouldn't want to talk about it.

The furrow on Trixin's forehead deepened. "She died last winter. When Brid was born." She shook her head. "She'd never had trouble birthing before, not even with the twins. And Brid came just fine, but then there was all this blood. . . . Da went for the midwife, but it was too late."

"I'm sorry," Raffa said.

"So am I," Trixin said. There was a spell of quiet, and then she looked at him with the usual snap and flash in her eyes. "She used to take in laundry and sewing, but I'm no good with a needle, so I had to find other work. Now it seems our luck has turned at last! This new job—I'll be able to buy shoes for the little ones, and a wrapper for the baby, and firewood for the whole winter, and who knows what else. I'd never have guessed it round about this time yesterday, but it's all thanks to you!"

"I didn't mean it," Raffa said. Which was true, and they both laughed.

"It is funny, isn't it," she said. "That we should meet on the street and end up working together."

Raffa nodded. He had known Trixin for only a day, yet he already felt at ease with her. Sheepishly, he remembered that, on first meeting her, he wished he had talked to someone else instead. Now he was glad he hadn't.

The apartments came into view, and Raffa trotted the rest of the way, with Trixin behind him. Courtyard, door, main room, Garith's bedroom . . . and there was Echo, hanging from the wall peg!

"Echo!" Raffa cried out. He rushed over, managing to restrain himself from grabbing the bat, whose claws were clenched tight in sleep. But he couldn't resist waking Echo by blowing on him gently.

"Echo, where have you been?" he murmured.

Chitter click hiss. Chitter hiss hissssss. Echo blinked balefully, the purple of his eyes glowing with annoyance.

Raffa didn't care—even the bat's grouchy sounds made him smile. "It's okay—you can tell me later. I'm so glad you're here. Go back to sleep now." He put the bat on the perch necklace under his tunic, vowing silently never again to be separated from him.

Trixin stood in the bedroom doorway, smiling at the reunion. "That's one done," she said. "Now all we have to do is find that bear for Kuma!"

With a shake of his head, Raffa corrected her. "You mean, find that bear *and* Kuma."

Where in the Commons could a bear possibly be hidden?

Fifth bell was ringing when Raffa and Trixin returned to the laboratory. Ansel was there with Garith.

"We found him!" Trixin announced.

Raffa tugged at the neckline of his tunic to let his uncle and cousin have a quick peek at the sleeping Echo. "When he's awake, I'll show you how well his wounds have healed," Raffa said.

"Let's hope the same for our little friends here," Ansel said, nodding toward the raccoons in their boxes on the shelf. He went on to say that while he had not found Kuma, a message was being sent to the guards and gatekeepers.

"I hope she returns of her own accord," Ansel said soberly. "If the guards have to bring her in, she could be regarded as having broken the terms of her service, which would almost certainly mean time in the Garrison."

"Oh, why is she being such a wobbler?" Trixin exclaimed.

Raffa had no idea what to do about Kuma. But he did know that he wanted to talk to Echo without anyone else around, and he still had to figure out how to be alone with the raccoons when they woke.

An idea came to him.

"Uncle Ansel, is it all right if I spend the night here, in the laboratory?" Raffa asked. "So I can keep an eye on the raccoons?"

"Why don't we take them to our quarters?" Garith suggested.

"No," Raffa said quickly. "I think they should be in the laboratory. In case anything happens in the middle of the night and they need to be treated."

"Should I stay with you?" Garith said—without much enthusiasm, Raffa noted. Despite their cooperation in working on the raccoons, it seemed that their disagreement was still ruffling the air.

"There's only the one bed," Ansel said. "The laboratory is intended for research, not treatment of patients."

"I don't mind staying on my own," Raffa said, hoping he sounded casual.

"That's decided, then," Ansel said. "Oh, and I nearly forgot—your parents sent the pigeon back today. Your mother has promised to help with the lying-in of Missum Kim. They will come for a visit after the baby is born, which should be in the next day or two."

Raffa was greatly relieved. It might just be possible to keep the secret of Echo's speech—and the raccoons' too, if that proved out—until his parents' arrival. The ache of missing them caught him unprepared. He could hardly believe it hadn't even been two days since he'd left home; it felt like much longer.

Trixin left with Garith and Ansel to go to the apartment, returning a while later with a blanket and a pannikin of dinner for Raffa. After one more look at the baby raccoons, she said her good-byes and went home.

Raffa ate his dinner, by which time it was dark outside. He washed his plate and mug, then pulled out the perch necklace.

"Don't talk, don't talk."

"It's okay, Echo. We're on our own here."

"Okay here, okay where?"

"We're at the pother laboratory," Raffa replied. He told Echo about the baby raccoons. "I'm going to wake them now."

He took the boxes off the shelf carefully, and uncovered the male raccoon. Bending over the box, he blew on its whiskers. The raccoon twitched, then batted its little front paws in front of its face.

Raffa held his breath. Would it speak?

The little beast woke with a cough and a splutter, followed by a pitiful mewl.

"Shusss, shusss," Raffa whispered soothingly. He was pleased to see the raccoon moving; it meant that the vine was indeed healing and curing again.

The raccoon looked right at Raffa, who noticed that its eyes were still dark; they hadn't yet taken on a purple sheen.

"Twig?" the raccoon said, in a small raspy voice. "Twig? Twig? Twig?"

Raffa didn't know whether to shout in triumph or groan in confusion: For the second time, the vine infusion had enabled an animal to speak!

"Twig? Twig?" the raccoon repeated, its voice now plaintive.

Why would a raccoon ask for a twig? It wasn't as if it needed a perch.

Garith's raccoon didn't respond when Raffa blew on her whiskers. Just as he began to worry, she too pawed and sniffed at the air, then gave a loud squeak.

The male raccoon responded immediately. "Twig!"

"Bando?" the female said weakly.

Each raccoon tried to move toward the other, but their injuries and the walls of their boxes prevented a reunion.

Echo was hanging from the shelf, watching with great interest. "Bando Twig," the bat said. "Bando Twig, Twig Bando."

"Mamma? Bando?"

"Twig! Twig!"

"Enough all of you! You're driving me ziggy!" Raffa said, putting his hands over his ears. "Just give me a minute, for quake's sake!"

Working carefully, he transferred the raccoons back to their original box so they could be together. Their joy and relief were palpable.

Using the dropper as Garith had shown him, he got the raccoons to take a little sweetened water. It was a temporary measure, at best. Raffa knew that no matter how well the twins healed, they would perish without their mother's milk. He wondered if a botanical substitute could be concocted, although he had never heard of such a thing. Maybe Uncle Ansel would know.

"Twig Bando, two pups born one," Echo said.

Raffa nodded. "Yes, I'm sure they're twins," he said.

Comforted by each other's presence, the little raccoons settled back to sleep, curled together as much as was possible with their bindings in the way.

With the laboratory now quiet, Raffa considered how he could keep the raccoons' speech a secret. Echo had heeded Raffa's warning not to talk in front of other people, but the raccoons were only babies; he didn't think he could count on them to do the same. Could he possibly hide them somewhere? But how would he explain their absence to Uncle Ansel?

Then Raffa heard a heartrending cry—not loud, but clearly desperate. It sounded very much like a baby. He rushed to the box to find Bando thrashing about in the throes of a bad dream. Both twins woke and began babbling.

"Bird," Bando said.

"Claw," his sister responded.

"Bird, bird!"

"Claw, claw!"

Now the raccoons were crying pitifully, and Echo squeaked several times in distress. The twins' words must have reminded the bat of his own wounding. Raffa frowned, wondering why he hadn't realized earlier how similar the raccoons' injuries were to Echo's. *Bird . . . claw . . .* Could the twins' injuries have been caused by a raptor, too?

"Bando Twig no good," Echo said. He moved to a spot on the shelf just above the box and hung with his head right above the raccoons. Then he chittered soothingly.

"No bird no claw," Echo said. "No bird no claw."

The raccoons looked up at Echo, who continued to chitter at them. The gentle sound calmed the baby twins.

Raffa stroked Echo's head fondly. "Thank you, Echo," he said.

He stood quietly, enjoying a rare moment of peace as Echo lulled the babies to sleep again. Then the bat fluttered back to the perch necklace.

"Now, tell me what happened to you," Raffa said, "starting when I left you last night—you were going to feed."

"Skeeto," Echo said. "Skeeto skeeto skeeto midge midge—"

"That's right. You went hunting in the courtyard."

"Perch sleep."

Raffa frowned. "So you *did* come in afterwards? But why weren't you there in the morning?"

"Friend Kuma."

"Kuma! What did she do, did she take you somewhere?"

"Echo go friend Kuma. Dark."

Raffa tried to hold the moving parts together in his mind. Echo had come in after hunting, before Raffa and the others were back from dinner at the Chancellor's. Then Kuma had fetched Echo away with her to go . . . where? Wherever it was, she had probably wanted Echo with her for his keen night senses.

"Echo, do you know where Kuma is now?"

"Kuma no good," Echo said.

Raffa was startled. What did that mean? Was Kuma in trouble? "What happened, Echo? Is she all right?"

Clicks and chitters.

"Oh, no. Echo, don't stop talking now!" He decided on another approach. "Could you take me to the last place you saw Kuma?"

Chitter, squeak, and then, "Echo go, Raffa come."

PART III

CHAPTER TWENTY-ONE

IT might have been wiser to wait until morning, but Raffa was too upset by the thought that Kuma might be in trouble. And even if she wasn't, he wanted to find her before she had a run-in with any of the guards.

The raccoons would surely be distressed if they woke to find themselves alone; they might thrash about and reopen their wounds. So he decided to bring them along.

After some thought, he used his leather rope and his rucksack to rig a sort of carrier that he strapped onto his front. He wrapped the raccoons in their box, which he put upright in the rucksack.

They both woke during these doings, but they were

calm now. Their little heads stuck out of the sack. Echo hung just above them on his perch. Raffa felt like the keeper of a traveling menagerie.

They started out, Echo guiding Raffa toward the north side of the Commons. As he walked, Raffa remembered something he wanted to discuss with the bat.

"Echo, do you like being able to talk?"

The bat was silent for so long that Raffa wondered if he had understood the question. He was debating whether he should ask again when finally Echo let out a little squeak.

"Echo Raffa talk good," the bat said. "Talk Raffa, talk Echo friends."

"You're a really good friend, Echo," Raffa said earnestly. "You and Garith are the best friends I've ever had." Then he checked himself—were he and Garith still friends? Surely a single argument couldn't sunder a lifelong friendship.

Or could it?

"Friend good," Echo said. "Raffa one, bats many."

With a throb in his gut, Raffa noticed that Echo did not sound happy. "You mean," he said slowly, "that you only have one human friend but lots of bat friends. And you miss them."

Echo chirped softly.

To Raffa's surprise, his eyes filled with tears. He wasn't sure why. Maybe it was because he now understood what it was like to be in an unfamiliar place, missing those closest to you. He had to swallow the lump in his throat before he could speak.

"I'll do my best to help you, Echo. If you decide you want to go back to living with bats again, maybe we can find an antidote to—to make you stop talking. If that's what you want."

Part of him—a very large part, maybe most of him— nearly cried out in protest. It wasn't what *he* wanted. If finding an antidote meant that Echo would leave him, he didn't even want to try.

He said none of this aloud. But it seemed that Echo sensed it anyway, for he reached up with one scarred wing and gently touched Raffa's chin.

Raffa checked frequently on the raccoons in the rucksack. With their wounds bound, he could not tell how well they were healing. But both were alert and apparently pain-free, and Bando had even managed to extricate one of his paws from its binding. Raffa tried to put the binding back on but couldn't manage in the dark.

Soon he smelled horses, and he realized that Echo had led him to the Commons stables. He followed the well-kept gravel drive, which even at this hour was illuminated by lanterns. More lanterns burned in the stable yard.

The stables were vast. He counted five buildings that held horses, each with two rows of stalls and a central alley wide enough for coaches or wagons. There were various outbuildings for tools and feed, as well as a huge smithy and a tack room as big as a barn.

It was quiet at this hour. Raffa heard the occasional nicker of a horse in its stall, but no one was moving about. He was puzzled: Was this their destination? Why would Kuma have gone to the stables?

"Raffa go," Echo said.

So it wasn't the stables. Keeping to the outer wall, he headed for the back of the stable yard. The pebbled drive here was not as grand or well-kept as the one leading to the front. The gate was open; Raffa crept up to it and peered around the edge.

Ten paces ahead, he saw a guard booth at the side of the drive. It looked to be unoccupied, but then Raffa heard a loud snore. He allowed himself a small smile: No need for a califerium combination this time.

"Quiet now," he whispered to Echo, who in turn clicked at the twins. He was fairly certain that the guard's job was to check on people entering the stable yard, not leaving it, but he was taking no chances.

He slipped past the sleeping guard and continued down the drive, which soon became a dirt track. The slums to the north of the Commons were supposedly even worse than those on the south side; he hoped he wouldn't have to go that far.

On both sides of the track lay a large expanse of over-grown land that served as sort of a buffer zone between the Commons and the slums. The light from the guard booth's lantern faded; it grew very dark, with only a clouded moon in the sky. Raffa's pace slowed. He took out the light stick, but its phosphorescence had dimmed to uselessness.

"Very near," Echo said then, to Raffa's relief. The bat directed him to turn left off the track.

Raffa continued walking far enough to know that the track would have disappeared from sight behind him. There was no path; he had to take one tentative step at a time to keep from stumbling.

Then Echo clicked sharply, and a large structure loomed out of the darkness in front of them.

A fence. A solid, heavy fence built higher than a man's head, and topped by boards studded with fierce nail points and broken glass. Its message was as clear as plain speech. *Keep out. You are not welcome.*

What was this place?

"Here, Echo? Kuma was here?" Raffa whispered.

"Kuma friend," Echo replied.

Raffa cautiously followed the fence until he came to a gate. Bolted shut from the inside, of course.

He glanced around nervously, reasoning that if the place was being guarded, sooner or later the guard would end up back here at the gate. He retraced his steps and decided to follow the fence in the other direction, to get some idea of its perimeter.

Raffa walked better than eighty paces before he reached the far corner of the fence. The enclosure was big enough to hold several buildings. He went back to the corner opposite the guard gate, figuring that from here he would be able to see someone approaching from two directions.

"Was she inside the fence, Echo?"

No reply. The fence being no barrier to Echo, *inside* and *outside* seemed at the moment to have no meaning to him.

Raffa kept hearing things—the rustle of leaves, the snap of a twig—but although he strained his eyes against the darkness, he saw no one. Ordinary noises could seem scarier in the dark, he thought, trying to reassure himself.

He took off the rucksack and set it carefully against the fence. The twins seemed to sense his tension and stayed quiet. A knothole, he thought. If he could find a knothole in one of the boards, he might be able to see what was inside the fence.

At Raffa's request, Echo left the perch necklace and alit on the fence above the rucksack to keep watch over the twins. Raffa had to walk nearly two-thirds the length of the fence again, but it was worth it. Better than a knothole: a crack between two boards.

Luck was with him: A breeze coaxed the clouds past the moon, and it was suddenly a little brighter. Raffa put his eye to the crack and peered into the enclosure.

People!

Not five paces away, on the other side of the fence!

He stifled a gasp and spun away in alarm, flattening himself against the boards. Had they heard him? Or maybe even seen the slight movement through the crack? He held his breath, which made his heart beat even faster. He listened as hard as he could through the pounding in his ears, and heard—

Nothing.

Utter silence, except for the rattle of leaves.

Raffa waited for what felt like three lifetimes. The silence held. He let out his breath an inch at a time, relief weakening his knees.

Then he closed his eyes tightly and counted to ten. It was a trick he often used when he wanted to see better in darkness, and this time it served to steady his nerves a little as well.

He opened his eyes and, moving as slowly as he could, turned and peeped through the crack again. Now he could see what he hadn't seen before.

Not people.

Scarecrows!

Nervous laughter bubbled up inside him, though he was quick to swallow it. What a fool he was, frightened out of his wits by a bunch of scarecrows.

Or something very like scarecrows, anyway. At least a half dozen that he could see, probably more, staked randomly throughout an open space. Each had a head and torso made from sacking stuffed with straw and mounted on posts.

The heads had crude faces: eyes and mouths that gaped black against the paler sacking. The breeze stirred the sacking, the clouds and moon cast formless moving shadows, and the scarecrows looked almost alive. . . .

Stop it, he told himself fiercely. It was bad enough being out here in the dark by himself without his imagination making things worse.

Why would anyone put up so many scarecrows where there was no grain or garden? Raffa stared at the scarecrow nearest him, searching for clues, but there didn't seem to be anything—

WHACK!

Something hard and flat walloped his upper back and neck. Raffa fell to his knees as little flecks of light swam in his vision.

He tried to get to his feet.

WHACK! Another blow, this time to the back of his legs. It hurt so much that he cried out in pain as he collapsed to his stomach on the ground.

Hardly knowing what he was doing, he covered his head with his arms. "Stop! Stop it!" he gasped.

To his amazement, he sensed the figure behind him go completely still. He rolled over onto his back and saw his attacker's silhouette against the veiled moonlight.

Not towering over him, as he had expected, but someone about his own size, holding what was apparently a wooden board.

He blinked.

"Kuma?" he said.

"Don't move or I'll hit you again," she said.

CHAPTER TWENTY-TWO

KUMA took a step toward him and raised the board over her shoulder, ready for another strike.

"I won't move, I swear!" Raffa said. "Kuma, what are you doing?"

"No, what are *you* doing?" Her voice was cold and hard. "Are you the one who did this?"

"Did what?" Raffa said. "I don't know what you're talking about! I came here to find you!"

"Your pother training," she said. "You could have done it. Or at least helped."

"Kuma, listen to me. I don't know what any of that means, but if I was the one who did . . . whatever it is you think I did, why would I be sneaking around in the middle of the night? And trying to look through the boards?"

Kuma made no move, and Raffa sensed her hesitation. He began to speak quickly. "Echo said 'Kuma no good,' so I was worried, and I asked him to show me the last place he'd seen you. He's over there"—Raffa pointed down the length of the fence—"you can ask him yourself."

Slowly Kuma lowered the board to the ground. Raffa waited a moment to make sure she wouldn't raise it again. Then he got to his feet, and began walking back toward the rucksack. After a few steps, he heard her following.

Echo flew to meet him, circled Kuma once, and alit on his perch. "Echo go, Raffa come, Kuma friend," he chirped.

"Thank you, Echo," Kuma said. She turned to Raffa. "I wasn't in any kind of trouble, but I've been . . . really upset. And sad. That must be why he said 'No good' about me."

The twins were hidden from view at first, but when they heard Raffa's footfalls, they popped their heads out, startling Kuma. "Oh!" she said softly, and dropped to her knees. She clucked at them, and they chirruped back at her.

Raffa told her about them—how they had been brought to the laboratory badly injured, and how he was treating them the same way he had treated Echo. After a pause, he said, "They can talk now, too."

With uncanny timing, Bando said, "Twig?"

Twig answered, "Bando?" Then in ragged chorus, they both said, "Mamma? Mamma? Mamma?"

Echo settled over them again and soothed them before they grew too agitated.

A long silence. Then Kuma stood and said, "I need to show you something. On the other side of the fence."

Raffa frowned. He didn't see how such an imposing fence could be scaled, and wasn't sure he wanted to even if it could. Nail points and broken glass—the place was unquestionably forbidden.

"Can't you just tell me?" he asked.

She shook her head. "You might not believe me. It's the kind of thing you have to see for yourself."

He hoped she would take his silence as a very firm *no*.

"I swear it's important," Kuma said. "The second you see it, you'll understand."

"But how—"

"This way." She started walking back along the fence.

Hastily Raffa picked up the rucksack and joined her. When they turned the corner, he saw a tree whose branches extended toward the fence but did not quite reach it.

"We have to wait until the guard passes on his rounds," Kuma whispered. "It should be soon enough."

"I'll leave the twins here," Raffa said, indicating the base of the tree. "Echo, will you stay and watch over them?"

"Bando Twig," Echo chirped.

It wasn't long before Kuma beckoned him. "I'll go first, so you can see how to do it," she said, and then she shinned up the tree. She went high, then higher still, until she was well above the level of the fence. Then she edged her way out onto a limb, which began to bend under her weight.

Watching from below, Raffa understood why she had climbed so high: The farther out she went on the limb, the more it sagged. At the point where he feared it would surely break underneath her, she leapt into the air and cleared the fence easily. Almost immediately, he heard a thump on the other side, so he guessed that she had landed on a roof rather than on the ground.

His turn now. He remembered scaling the rock wall

in the underground passage with Trixin and, before that, climbing the querco tree in the Forest to get the red vine. Why did there always have to be something to climb?

Trying to copy Kuma's exact movements, he held on to a branch overhead as he slid his feet along the limb, which shook and bounced alarmingly. In what seemed to be an act of concern, Echo left his perch over the twins and began circling nearby.

"Raffa fly?" he squeaked. Raffa would have laughed if he hadn't been so frightened.

He could now see over the fence, where Kuma awaited him on a roof that—mercifully—had only a slight pitch. He did not allow himself time to think; if he did, he knew he would never let go of the limb.

He launched himself into the air.

The roof hit him much sooner than he expected. His breath was jarred from his lungs as he landed half on his feet, half on his side. Before he could stop himself, he was rolling off the edge of the roof. Frantically he scrabbled for the eaves; they slipped from his grasp, but he managed to hold on long enough to slow his fall.

"Huff!" he grunted as he landed on the ground. Still breathless, he looked around in a panic. Had the guard heard him? He couldn't seem to quiet his breath;

it sounded as loud as thunder to him.

Kuma dropped down beside him, silent as a cat.

Too late, Raffa wondered how they would get out; they couldn't go back the way they came. "How do we get out of here?" he panted.

"You'll see," Kuma whispered. "It's a bit trickier."

Trickier than what they'd just done? Lovely.

Kuma led him around the back of the shed to an identical building. Keeping close to the wall, she edged her way to the door, which was latched but not locked. She unhooked the latch and held the door open for him.

Raffa stepped inside. It was so dark that he couldn't see his hand in front of his face. But he could smell and hear—and feel, even though he wasn't touching anything.

Animals. He smelled them: breath and fur and waste. The space was filled with animals, all completely, eerily silent. How was that possible? They should have woken, at least some of them, when Kuma opened the door.

Moving slowly, carefully, Raffa stepped with his hands out in front of him. Then stripes of moonlight entered the shed through slats in the ceiling, and for a few moments, he could see.

Shelves lined three of the four walls, from floor to

ceiling, with more rows of shelves filling the shed's interior. Each shelf held dozens of small cages, and each cage held an animal. Their limbs were splayed or twitching in a deep but unnatural sleep, which meant that they had been dosed with a sedative.

And every single one of them was a baby.

Raffa saw foxes and badgers. Others were small balls of fur that he couldn't distinguish in the dim light.

Clouds masked the moon again. Raffa stood in the darkness, stunned at what he had just seen. The animals were weeks old, at most—too young to be taken from their mothers. Where were all the mothers?

Kuma tugged on his sleeve. "There are eleven more sheds just like this," she whispered.

Twelve sheds. Hundreds of animals altogether. Who had captured them? And how had they managed to amass so many?

Then Raffa remembered the clearing that he and Garith had seen in the Forest. No, not a clearing—a camp. Whoever it was, they could have been there for weeks, hunting down every baby animal or pregnant mother within miles. It was only a guess, but he was shaken by how well it fitted.

He tried to remember what the Chancellor had said at

dinner about the project. Training animals to do the work of humans . . . What sort of human work could foxes and badgers do that would call for so many of them?

As he and Kuma left the shed, Raffa looked around quickly. "Did you see the scarecrows?" he asked tensely.

"Yes," Kuma said. "I'll tell you later. Stick close now. We're going out through the gate. It's bolted from the inside. We have to watch for the guard to leave on his next round, then make a run for it."

It sounded simple enough. Staying close to the fence, they passed the scarecrows in a large space between two sheds. Then they walked nearly the whole length of the compound. Kuma stopped at the second to last shed. "This is the only one with adult animals," she said. "And the last one is empty."

They slipped behind the last shed. Kuma gestured for Raffa to peep around its wall. From there he could see the gate, and a small hut with the guard seated inside.

To Raffa's dismay, there was nothing but open ground between them and the gate. A lantern shone brightly from the hut. Even after the guard began his rounds, all he would have to do was turn his head and he would see them.

"I did it before," Kuma breathed. "We just have to be

really quick. When you get out, go to the right, beyond the end of the fence, and duck down in the brush."

It seemed like half the night before the guard finally rose and left the hut, holding another lantern. Kuma waited until he had walked a few dozen paces away. "Ready?" she said.

Raffa was about to nod in response when he heard Echo chirp overhead. What was he doing here? Raffa saw the bat fly straight toward the guard and land on the ground, at the edge of the circle of lantern light.

Quick as a blink, Kuma clapped her hand over Raffa's mouth, stifling his cry. He yanked her hand away.

"We can't leave now!" he said in an anguished whisper. "I won't go without him!"

Kuma hissed at him for silence. Raffa shouldered her out of the way and watched in dismay as Echo flap-staggered out of the light.

"A bat?" the guard said, his voice carrying through the still air. "Dirty thing. What are you doing down there? Must be hurt, are you?"

He moved toward Echo. With each step he took, Echo flapped and hopped a bit farther away, staying in sight but out of reach.

Suddenly Raffa recalled the partridge he had seen

years before, which had feigned injury to draw him away from her nest. He turned to Kuma, his eyes shining with excitement. "He's distracting the guard for us!"

Kuma was already moving. When they reached the gate, she slid back the bolt. Raffa gave the gate a push—and pushed too hard. It swung fully open and banged against the fence.

They were outside the gate in a flash, both running as fast as they could. The guard shouted and began chasing them. When Raffa reached the stretch of scrubland, he plunged on blindly until he crashed into a thicket of shrubs and flipped heels skyward over it. He landed on his back, rolled over, and froze. A moment later, Kuma threw herself down beside him.

The guard pursued them as far as the end of the fence. Raffa heard his heavy footfalls stop. The guard held his lantern high and moved it in a semicircle; its beam of light swept so close that Raffa could have touched it.

The light swung by again, more slowly, and Raffa would have sworn it was even closer this time. It took every fiber of his nerve not to flee.

Finally the guard muttered angrily and stomped back to the gate. Still they waited—to hear the gate close and the bolt being shot home again. Then Kuma got to her hands and knees. She crawled for several yards before rising to a cautious crouch, and Raffa followed her lead.

They tiptoed back to the tree to fetch the twins, then made their way to the track that led to the stable yard, where Echo rejoined them with his usual "Ouch" on landing. Raffa gave him a quick stroke of silent thanks.

Slipping past the still-sleeping stable guard felt like a toddler's game after what they had been through. Raffa was so exhausted that he had to concentrate just to keep his feet moving. It seemed like the walk would never end.

When at last they reached the laboratory, he led Kuma to the tiny bedchamber and shuttered the window. Only then did he light a lantern.

He left the twins in the rucksack; they had fallen asleep again on the long walk back to the laboratory. He hung Echo's perch on a wall peg. Then he drew out his waterskin, drank thirstily, and handed it to Kuma.

By the time she finished drinking, his pulse was almost back to normal. "Tell me everything there is to tell," he said.

Kuma leaned back against the wall and started talking.

CHAPTER TWENTY-THREE

"THEY used a wagon when they took her. Roo, I mean."

"Your bear," Raffa said.

Kuma glared at him. "She's not *mine*. Any more than Echo is *yours*."

Her words brought Raffa up short. He realized that in his fondness for Echo, the bat had come to feel almost like a pet. But like Roo, Echo wasn't tame; he could leave whenever he chose. As much as that thought pained him, it also served to deepen his wonder that a wild creature was spending time with him.

He nodded slowly, and she went on. "So, because of

the wagon, I thought that the horses might have ended up back at the stables. I couldn't think of anywhere else to look. I left last night, while you were at dinner."

"You took Echo." Now Raffa's voice was cold. He could not forget his panic when he found that Echo was missing—nor forgive her for being the cause of it. She of all people should have understood how upset he would be.

"It was dark, and . . . I didn't want to go alone," she confessed. "I swear I kept him in sight the whole time. I made sure nothing happened to him. Later, around sunpeak, he insisted on leaving. 'Raffa perch,' he kept saying, so I let him go. I'm sorry, I couldn't think of any way to let you know."

Raffa said nothing, but it made him feel better to know that Echo had been thinking of him. He looked at the bat, who was busy grooming himself.

Kuma waited for a moment, then continued. "I found that place. And figured out a way to get in. It wasn't hard—in the Forest I climb a lot.

"I stayed inside the fence most of the day. Servients are working there. I saw them go in and out of the sheds. But it's a big place, it was easy to stay hidden. And they left the doors unlatched while they were working. So I peeked into all the sheds and saw . . . well, you know."

Then her shoulders slumped. "Roo's not there. None of the cages are anywhere near big enough to hold her."

"If they're the ones who took her, then she's alive," Raffa said, "I'm sure of it. They don't want to kill these animals—they want to train them."

"To do what?" Kuma's voice trembled with trepidation.

Raffa paused, considering the kinds of tasks an animal as big and strong as a bear might be able to manage. A thought crossed his mind: night slopping. What Trixin's father did. Lifting the heavy barrels of human waste, emptying them into the vats . . . Could a bear do that?

"Whatever it is, I can't believe for one moment that she would stand for it," Kuma was saying. "She never lets anyone but me get near her."

Raffa blinked as realization dawned. "That's it," he said, his voice low but certain. "That's why they gave you a term of service. They know about you and Roo—just like I did, I'd heard about you before I came here. They want you to help them train her."

They.

The Chancellor. And whoever was working for her. Who else? Did the project have the approval of the Advocate, holder of the highest office in Obsidia? And even more important to Raffa, what about Uncle Ansel and Garith? His mind balked. Surely his uncle and cousin didn't know about the shed compound and all those imprisoned baby animals; they would never have agreed to engage in something so cruel.

Kuma sat up, her eyes blazing. "I won't do it! They can't make me!"

Raffa looked away, not wanting to say what he was thinking. They *could* make her, and it wouldn't even be hard. All they would have to do was threaten to hurt the bear if Kuma didn't cooperate.

The same thought must have occurred to her, for she gave a bone-shaking shudder.

Raffa touched her arm. "If I'm right, you don't have to search for her anymore. They'll bring her to you. Or you to her. You need to go to my uncle in the morning and—and apologize for disappearing. Once we know where she is, we'll figure out a plan."

He furrowed his brow, remembering something he wanted to ask about that would also serve to take Kuma's mind off Roo for at least a few moments. "Those scarecrows . . . you said you'd tell me about them."

"Oh. They were just there. I didn't see anyone doing

anything with them. But here's a strange thing: grapes. On the ground around the scarecrows. A whole lot of grapes, crushed or half-eaten."

Grapes? Raffa didn't think he'd ever in his life been more puzzled.

At that moment, one of the twins began sobbing in its sleep. It was only a tiny noise, but it was one of the saddest sounds Raffa had ever heard.

"Mamma . . . Mamma . . ."

Echo flapped from his perch to the rucksack. "Twig sleep, sleeeep," the bat said soothingly. He seemed to be able to tell the twins apart as easily as their mother would.

Raffa had a sudden thought. "Kuma! The animals in that one shed, the adults—are they mostly female?"

She was startled at first, then frowned in concentration. "They might be. . . . Yes, I think they are. A lot of them, anyway."

Raffa rapped himself on the head in frustration. "Why didn't I think of it when we were there! They'd have to keep the mothers around until the babies are weaned, right? The mother raccoon might be in that shed!"

Echo flitted back to his perch, having once again

accomplished his duties as the twins' nanny. Raffa took the raccoons' box out of the rucksack—and Kuma's eyes grew wide with alarm.

"That box," she said, staring at it hard.

"What about it?" He looked at it curiously. It was an ordinary wooden box, the one that had held the raccoons when Trixin first brought them to the laboratory.

"I saw it, this morning. I didn't know—but you said—" She pressed her hands against her stomach, as if bracing herself.

Raffa couldn't fathom why she found the box so upsetting.

Kuma swallowed hard. "Two men. One was carrying that very box. I could swear it. They passed right by where I was hiding. It was covered—I couldn't see what was inside, but now I know—it must have been the raccoons. They went into one of the sheds, the empty one. And then a third man took something else inside."

"What was it?" Raffa asked.

"I—I—I'm not sure. But the way he was carrying it . . ." She held her arm out away from her body, her hand in a fist and her forearm parallel to the ground. "There was a—a sort of bag over it. And he was wearing a big glove."

"A raptor," Raffa said slowly. "An owl. Or maybe a hawk."

A shaft of ice seemed to run up his spine. He could not stop the awful images that filled his mind's eye. The two men taking the baby raccoons into the shed. A third man carrying a raptor inside.

The raptor's hood being removed, its jesses untied, and then—

The *whoosh* of the sleek feathered wings in terrible contrast to the tortured cries of little Bando and Twig as the raptor attacked them with beak and claw, again and again and again . . .

For a moment Raffa thought he might get sick. It was one thing for predators to hunt their prey in the wild. This attack in an enclosed space on totally defenseless babies—this was something else altogether.

He had to take several breaths before he could speak again. "Who were the men? Did you know them?"

Kuma shook her head.

"What did they look like? Do you remember anything more about them?"

She scowled in concentration. "The first two . . . One was taller than the other. And the shorter one was darker. The third man . . . I couldn't see his face. He was wearing a hood, but I remember thinking that he looked sort of—I don't know—raggedy compared to the other two."

"Raggedy?"

"His clothes. Maybe I'm wrong." She shrugged hopelessly. "I didn't know I should be paying more attention to them. I was only thinking of Roo."

Raffa's mind was still staggered by the horror of it. Why would anyone want to maim two tiny baby raccoons?

So many questions. How could he possibly decide what to do next when he had so few answers?

"Kuma, I have to talk to my uncle. He must know some things we don't. And if he doesn't—if he's being kept in the dark about the way the raccoons got hurt, and about all those other baby animals—then he needs to know, and maybe he'll be able to—"

"No!" Kuma's voice could not have been more emphatic. "You can't tell him anything! What if he's part of it? They're obviously trying to keep everything secret, and if you tell him what we know, they're sure to stop us from finding out anything else!"

"He's not part of it. You don't know him, he would never—"

"That's right." Kuma cut him off, her eyes flashing. "I don't know him, so how can I trust him? I don't even know *you* very well, and there's only one reason I'm trusting you."

She flicked a glance at Echo, hanging on his perch. "Because *he* does. People are . . . They're tricky. They lie, you can't depend on them. Animals are more reliable, if you ask me."

"My uncle would never do anything to hurt me."

A pause. "I don't mean to speak ill of your family," Kuma said. "But Roo is—she's like *my* family. I have to get her out of here."

"But we can't handle this alone," Raffa said. "It's too—too big."

Kuma sat up straighter. "Alone? We're not alone, either of us. You'll have my help and I'll have yours, and that's way more than I usually have."

"What about Garith? He's been here for a while now, he knows his way around. Maybe he could help—"

"Do you trust him not to say anything to your uncle?"

Raffa started to say yes, but the word lodged in his throat. The disagreement with Garith had been their worst ever. Raffa wasn't sure how Garith would react to anything he said.

"That leaves Trixin," Kuma said. "But I don't think we should ask her to help us."

"Why not?" Raffa liked Trixin. She may have been too outspoken at times, but it was part of her honesty, and beneath her impatience, he sensed that she was steady upon solid.

"She works for your uncle," Kuma said. "We can't ask her to hide anything from him. If she gets caught, she might lose her job, and you know she can't afford for that to happen."

Raffa felt guilty that he hadn't thought of this himself.

Silence. Echo chirped softly, as if aware of the seriousness of the conversation. Raffa reached for him and stroked his back.

"The most important thing to me," Kuma said at last, "is finding Roo and freeing her. If you're right about my service assignment, I'll be working with Roo. That's step one taken care of. And once I'm with her, I'll figure out a way to free her. If I can't stop you from talking to your uncle, then at least don't give me away. Is that fair enough?"

Raffa did not reply at once. Nothing about this was fair.

But what if he were in Kuma's place, and it was Echo he was trying to free? Raffa looked down at the bat, who stared back at him and chirped again.

That made the decision easy.

"Fair enough," he said with a nod.

CHAPTER TWENTY-FOUR

RAFFA felt like he had only just closed his eyes when he was awakened by the sound of the laboratory door opening. He found himself on the floor with his head on the chair.

"Raffa?" Uncle Ansel's voice.

Another voice: "Maybe he's not awake yet." Garith.

"Sleepydeep, I've been up for hours!" Trixin.

Raffa staggered to his feet. "I'm just coming," he said, his voice rusty.

Kuma sat up on the bed. She rubbed her eyes, then opened them wide. Pushing aside the blanket, she picked up the box with the raccoons, who had begun to stir.

"Good luck," she whispered, to both Raffa and the twins.

Before going to sleep, Raffa had considered one more problem: how to keep the twins' ability to speak a secret. With Echo's help, the twins had been made to understand that a raptor—*the* raptor, the bird that had attacked them—was going to be in the vicinity, and that they had to stay absolutely still and silent.

It was an awful thing to do to them, but Raffa hadn't been able to think of anything else short of dosing them with a sedative, which he refused to do.

He put on the perch necklace, tucked it under his tunic, and took the box from Kuma. She stood and exchanged one last look with him. Then he pushed open the door of the bedchamber.

"Steady morning," he called out, hoping he sounded cheerful. He had decided not to ask his uncle about the shed compound until after Kuma had been reunited with Roo, worried that he might somehow give away her plans. For the moment, he had to act as if nothing was amiss. "Look who came to see me!"

Kuma stepped forward and bowed her head toward Ansel. "Senior Vale, I am truly sorry," she said. "I just—I lost my head. I wasn't thinking straight. I was so worried about Roo that I had to go and look for her. Raffa told me it was wrong of me not to tell you, and I see that now. I promise it won't happen again."

Raffa was watching his uncle closely. Ansel's expression went from surprise on first seeing Kuma through a quick frown of anger, before finally settling into grudging acceptance.

He nodded once. "I am glad I did not have to ask for an apology," he said, "and I'm sure you will understand that until you have proved yourself reliable, you will not be allowed to go anywhere on your own."

"I do understand," Kuma said quietly.

"All right, then," Ansel said, and nodded again. "We'll say no more about it for the moment. Raffa, what of the raccoons?"

Raffa put the box down on the worktable, holding his breath.

"They're awake," Garith said. "But look at them— they're scared to death."

Bando and Twig were curled into tight little balls, their faces not even visible. Their violent trembling was the only indication that they were awake. Ansel bent over the box. He touched Twig with a fingertip, trying to provoke a response. The raccoon curled up still tighter.

Raffa's idea was working, but the obvious terror of the little raccoons tore at his heart. He hoped everyone else would leave for at least part of the day, so he could tell the babies that the fictional raptor had flown off.

"Well, clearly their wounds are healing well," Ansel said, after taking a look under Twig's bindings. "That vine may be a miracle plant, but cheers also to the pother." He smiled at Raffa, who quickly held his hands out toward Garith for a celebratory clap, including him in the credit.

"The work goes on," Ansel said. "Kuma, I am especially relieved at your return because you are to start your service this afternoon."

"Senior Vale, may I ask what I will be doing?" Kuma's voice was so polite that Raffa was sure he was the only one who heard the tension in it.

"It would be much better to wait until I can show you," Ansel answered. "Please, don't worry. For now, Trixin can accompany you to the apartment. You can wash and rest a little, until lunchtime."

Trixin looked disappointed. "Are you sure you don't need me to pickle anything?" she asked.

Ansel chuckled. "Not at the moment. Later today I'm expecting a crate of sea-celery, and we'll want some of it pickled. So you have that to look forward to."

The girls departed. Ansel watched them leave, then turned to Raffa. "Now, some good news," he said. "I did not want to mention it with Kuma here, as you will understand in a moment. . . . The bear has been found!"

"What?"

"Where?"

"How big is it?"

"Is she all right?"

Ansel raised his hand to stem the flood of excited babble from the boys. "The bear is now safely in Senior Jayney's care. He is not certain if the beast can be part of the project, but it is the Chancellor's wish that we at least make an attempt."

"But why couldn't you tell Kuma right away?" Raffa asked.

"As you can imagine, the bear is rather distressed," Ansel replied. "Kuma would doubtless have insisted on seeing it immediately, and I thought it would upset her to see it in that state. Senior Jayney has requested an infusion that will calm the bear, yet leave it alert enough to assess its potential for training."

Raffa kept his face steady. Kuma would be wild with dismay over any notion of dosing Roo, even if the effects were only temporary.

"What about the combination we've been using?" Garith suggested.

Ansel shook his head. "The bear would have to drink bucketsful for it to have the desired effect. Raffa, we need a similar infusion, but both more concentrated and more powerful. Do you think you can do it?"

Raffa saw Garith's shoulders stiffen, and he knew what his cousin was thinking. *Raffa this, Raffa that . . .* It wasn't fair to Garith. He had been doing good work here; Uncle should at least have asked them both.

"Garith is the one who's been making the training infusion," Raffa said. "He knows it best. I think we should work on it together."

Ansel deliberated for a moment. "Fine," he said. "You can begin together, but Garith will need to leave at third bell to dose the trainees, so it is likely that you will finish on your own." A pause. "I am going to report that you did a fine job on the raccoons, but another success would be all to the good."

Raffa lowered his head. The garble with the crow had been his own doing, but it still rankled that anyone, even the Chancellor with her loathsome project, should think so little of his pothering.

"I have to prepare a stimulant infusion requested by Senior Jayney," Ansel continued. "It will be a busy morning, so we need to get started. Raffa, have you had breakfast?"

While Raffa hastily downed an oatcake from the laboratory's small pantry, Garith laid out the ingredients for the training infusion. "Califerium and millocham," he muttered, "plus the vine."

Garith seemed more than a little sulky, and Raffa hoped he and his cousin might have some time alone to steady things left wobbled by yesterday's argument. He took up a place cornerwise from Garith at the table.

Their first task would be to modify the amounts of the botanicals to account for the bear's size and weight. "What's the biggest animal that's had the infusion so far?" Raffa asked.

Garith considered for a moment. "Stoats, maybe? I dosed them yesterday."

Stoats . . . Raffa had seen the weasel-like creatures a few times on the outskirts of the Forest. They were both fierce and unfriendly, sharp of teeth and claw; a less cuddly creature was hard to imagine. "What are they being trained to do?" he wondered aloud.

Garith shrugged. "I don't know. We make the

infusions and dose the animals. Senior Jayney is the one in charge of the training."

Raffa tensed slightly and tried to keep his voice casual. "Do you ever get to watch? Sounds like it might be kind of fun."

"No, Da says an audience would be distracting. Wait—I just remembered. We dosed badgers a few days ago—they're bigger than stoats."

There followed a lengthy discussion on the relative weights of bears and badgers and how that would affect the amounts of the ingredients for the infusion. Raffa was terrible with figures; after only a few attempts, he flipped away his piece of chalk. "I'm toppled," he said in disgust.

"I've almost got it," Garith declared. "Steady on for one more sec—okay, here it is. You'd better check it over."

Raffa worked Garith's figures backwards. Everything came out as it should. As they began to prepare the infusion, Raffa realized that it was the first time in what seemed like weeks that he was having fun. This was his idea of what apothecary should be—working on a challenge, in a place where he had everything he needed, and with Garith in better humor as well.

They stood side by side now, between the stove and the table. Garith did the measuring and handed the ingredients to Raffa, who combined them carefully. As he added the vine pulp, the silent hum suffused his mind. It was somehow deeper than before; he thought it might be in response to the more concentrated intensity of the combination.

Then they heard the ring of the Commons bells. "Third bell," Garith said. "I have to dose the animals now."

"Where do you go for that?" Raffa asked.

"There's a place out back of the stables," Garith said vaguely. "Mannum Trubb brings the animals to me there. I'll be back before lunchtime."

"Mmm," Raffa said. "I'll keep on here, then."

His mind was racing. Garith obviously knew about the shed compound. Surely he also had to know about the hundreds of baby animals! How could he possibly—

Then Raffa remembered the last shed. The empty one. That had to be where Garith did the dosing. . . . Maybe he wasn't aware of what was inside the other sheds. Raffa knew that this might well be more hope than sense, but he had no way of asking about it without revealing his nighttime venture.

After Garith departed, Raffa put a kettle of water on to boil, then began collecting the equipment he would need to make the infusion. Uncle Ansel continued working on the other side of the laboratory. From outside came the sounds of hoofbeats slowing and wagon wheels creaking to a stop, and then a voice as someone hailed Ansel.

"That will be Jayney," Ansel said. "He won't come in. He says all the magic in the room makes him jibbery." He rolled his eyes, and in return, Raffa grinned and shrugged. But his nerves went taut, like a deer on alert.

Jayney. The man in charge of training the animals. Whatever he had to say, Raffa wanted to hear it.

Ansel wiped his hands on a cloth. "I'll just go and speak to him."

As soon as his uncle stepped outside, Raffa hurried into the bedchamber, which had the window closest to the laboratory door. He eased open the shutter the merest crack.

"—the Afters live everywhere, not just the slums," Jayney was saying.

"My only concerns are the infusions," Ansel replied. "The bear's will be ready for this afternoon."

"Good," Jayney said. "The Chancellor knows as well

as we do that the bear has the potential to make us all but invincible."

Invincible? Raffa frowned in bewilderment and listened all the harder.

"A pity there aren't two of them," Jayney went on. "I have been thinking that it would be good to have wolves for the other front, and have raised the bounty for a wolf set."

"It may take some time to adjust the infusion for the bear," Ansel said.

"Hmph. And the stimulant for the stoats and badgers?"

"It's finished. I'll come with you and dose them myself. I'll be but a moment."

Raffa scrambled back into the main room and made it to the stove, where he began fussing with the drafts as Ansel entered.

"I'm working with Senior Jayney for the next while," Ansel said. "Take a break for lunch, won't you?" He smiled at Raffa.

"I'll do that," Raffa said, a little too loudly. He could feel his face reddening and hoped that, if Ansel noticed, he would think it because of the heat from the stove.

Ansel cleaned up his work area quickly, then departed.

Raffa was alone now; he felt his neck and shoulders relax a little. He hadn't realized how tight they were.

First matters first: Raffa checked on the twins. Mercifully, they had fallen asleep, and he hoped they would sleep the whole day. Without waking them, he looked under their bindings. The wounds were healing beautifully. As he bent over the raccoons, he tried to make sense of the conversation he had just heard.

Invincible. That wasn't a word you would use when training animals to do tasks. And Jayney had mentioned wanting wolves. A bear, wolves, stoats, badgers—all fierce and fearsome. Maybe the animals were for fighting; in that case, the desire to be invincible would make sense.

But against what enemy? Ever since the Great Quake had isolated Obsidia from neighboring lands, its people had lived without fear of invasion. It was so unlikely that Raffa almost cast aside the entire notion.

Then one of the twins grumbled in its sleep, and he stared down at them with a throb of dreadful realization. If you were preparing for a battle, the ability to heal grave injuries quickly would be a tremendous advantage. Had Bando and Twig been the subjects of some terrible experiment?

Raffa shuddered, then groaned inwardly. The more he learned about the project, the less he seemed to know.

The door opened. Trixin and Kuma had returned.

"How are they doing?" Kuma asked.

"Much better," Raffa answered as he covered the raccoons' box with a cloth.

"We brought lunch," Trixin said, and began unpacking a flat basket. "I hope you're hungry, we've enough to feed a crowd. That pantry at the Vales' apartment—it's a wonder! Two kinds of cheese, both bread *and* farls— oh, we forgot to bring plates. There must be some here somewhere."

She bustled into the small pantry and came out again a moment later. "Mugs, but no plates," she said. "Kuma, will you check that closet?"

Kuma turned and opened a narrow closet near the door. Raffa was close enough to hear her strangled gasp. He saw her freeze, still as a stone for a long moment.

"Any plates?" Trixin called from across the room where she was pouring water from the kettle into a teapot.

Kuma cleared her throat. "No—no plates," she said. Slowly she moved her head until she could meet Raffa's gaze. "Nothing in here but this—this *raggedy* old thing."

Now it was Raffa's turn to freeze. *Raggedy.* She had

used that word before . . . to describe the man who had taken the raptor into the shed to torture the twins.

Kuma pulled something from the closet and held it out toward him, her hands shaking.

It was Uncle Ansel's old leather tunic.

CHAPTER TWENTY-FIVE

THE room spun, and Raffa gripped the edge of the table. In a last throb of desperation, he tried to tell himself that someone else could have been wearing the tunic. But that thought fell apart in shreds as tattered as the tunic itself.

Uncle Ansel had hurt Bando and Twig on purpose. And lied about it. He knew everything. No, worse than that: He was *part* of everything.

It was the simplest answer. Nothing else explained all the mysteries. Through the whirl in his brain, he heard Trixin from somewhere far away: "Raffa, are you all right?"

"I'm fine," he heard himself say. "Just . . . um, a little tired."

Trixin poured out a mug of tea, stirred in some honey, and handed it to him. "Sit down and drink that," she ordered.

Raffa obeyed as if he were dreamwalking. But the hot, sweet tea helped steady him.

He had to leave. Had to get away from his uncle, go home and tell his parents everything. He wanted to feel his mother's arms around him, hear her wise and funny words. He even wanted his father's sternness, which felt like something solid, something he could lean on.

Not in a few days. *Now.*

"Did your uncle say when he'd be back?" Kuma asked, and he knew she had asked the question in an attempt to steady him.

"No," he answered woodenly. "But I think it should be soon."

With those words, his reason snapped back to life.

Roo.

Ansel would be taking Kuma to Roo—almost certainly to the shed compound. Raffa was supposed to have the infusion ready to dose the bear. The flicker of an idea came to him. It grew into a flame, and quickly, for he had very little time.

He jumped to his feet and hurried to the stove, where the solution he had made with Garith was simmering. "I'm going to finish this up now," he said loudly. "You two just go ahead and eat. It won't take me long."

And it didn't, because there was no need for precise calculations or careful measurements. Raffa waited until the girls had their backs to him, then took the beaker of solution and emptied it out the window. Standing at the counter, he quickly mixed honey and water in the beaker. In the large cabinet he found the drawer holding dried quagberries.

He steeped the berries, crushed them, and strained them into the beaker to turn the honey mixture red—not the exact shade of the scarlet vine infusions, but close enough. Then he poured the liquid from the glass beaker into an earthenware jar, which made the color harder to discern.

Raffa corked the jar. Finished.

He had made a "cinder"—an infusion both harmless and useless.

Raffa went into the bedchamber. He donned Echo's perch necklace; the bat sleep-grumbled at the disturbance but settled again under Raffa's tunic. He took the twins out of the box, swaddled them well in soft rags, and put them in a hemp bag. Then he hurried to the laboratory's small pantry, where he packed all the edibles he could find into his rucksack.

In the glasshouse, he gathered up the clippings of the scarlet vine, wrapping them in damp cloths, and put them in the rucksack, too. He was nearly ready: The only thing he needed now was a chance to speak to Kuma alone.

The color in his cheeks was high as he returned to the laboratory and sat down for a quick bite to eat. Trixin shook her head. "What's in you today—one minute you can hardly stand up straight; the next you're running around all ziggy!"

"Er—it must have been the tea," Raffa said. "Did you put something in it? Are you turning pother already?"

He was relieved when she giggled. "Of course not," she said. "It's just zinjal and mint!" Trixin, at least, didn't seem to suspect anything.

The door opened and Garith came in.

"Is there any more food?" he asked. "Da sent me to fetch you all. He said to come right away. Are you going to eat that?" He pointed to the farl in front of Raffa, who handed it over.

Garith took a big bite. "Don't forget the infusion," he

said. He grabbed a handful of dried plums. "Let's go."

Raffa lagged behind, hoping to talk to Kuma, but she and Trixin promptly followed Garith out of the laboratory to the lane, where a wagon awaited them. Garith sat up front with the driver, with the others on the bench behind.

Raffa's mind was in a whirl. He couldn't make his plan work without Kuma, but it was too late to speak to her alone. He would have to think of some other way. . . .

The wagon took the route toward the shed compound. Trixin, seated next to him, gave his arm a nudge. "Shakes, you look serious," she said, her voice loud over the wagon's rattling wheels. "Anything I can do to help?"

Raffa found himself touched by her concern. "I wish there was," he mumbled.

"What? Speak up, won't you?"

"It's nothing," he said, and managed to give her a small smile.

Then Garith turned his head toward them. "Almost there," he said.

The wagon drove through the gate of the compound, where a small cluster of people were standing: Ansel, two other men, and the Chancellor.

Kuma nudged Raffa with an elbow, and he saw her gaze flick over the two men. One was tall and pale, with a beaky nose; the other was dark and bearded and solidly built. They were surely the men she had seen with Ansel and the baby raccoons. The tall one was carrying a spiked bluggen.

Raffa gulped. He hadn't counted on the presence of weapons.

"Welcome!" Ansel called as the foursome climbed down from the wagon.

Raffa's nerves strained as he forced himself to look at his uncle. He almost expected that Ansel would have glaring red eyes now, or at the very least a noxious leer. But he looked the same as always, like the man Raffa had always thought of as a second father. His stomach lurched again.

"Greetings," Chancellor Leeds said. She smiled warmly at all of them, then looked directly at Raffa. "Young Santana, your uncle has told me of your fine work healing—what was it, raccoons? I am more than pleased."

Raffa bowed over his fists, which were properly joined—and tightly clenched. "Thank you, Chancellor," he mumbled, not trusting his voice enough to speak any louder.

The Chancellor indicated the two men. "Senior Jayney and Mannum Trubb have charge of the animal training," she said, "and as such have been working closely with Senior Vale and young Vale. Senior Jayney, you wish to speak to our newcomers?"

The dark burly man stepped forward. "Most of this compound will not concern you," he said. "Indeed, any disruption would be unacceptable. Your work will be confined to the first shed." Pause. "I am sure I will have no cause to regret your presence here."

Raffa recognized the voice he had heard talking to Uncle Ansel. Jayney sounded laconic, almost lazy, but Raffa shivered to hear him.

"Let's get started," said Mannum Trubb, whose words seemed to come out through his nose. "Sooner begun, sooner done."

Jayney nodded. Ansel rubbed his hands together. "Now, then, Kuma," he said, and Raffa saw her straighten in alertness. "I have wonderful news for you! The bear has been found—and it is here."

Kuma gasped and dropped her face into her hands for a moment; when she looked up again, her cheeks were shining with tears. "Please," she said, "can I see her?"

"We shall do much better than that," Ansel said, smiling broadly. "For your service assignment, you will be with her every day." He beckoned Kuma, and they began walking toward the shed, with the rest of the group trailing.

"There is no need for alarm," Ansel said. "But as you can imagine, the bear has been in something of a distressed state. The first thing to be done, I'm sure you will agree, is to calm and soothe her. Raffa has made an infusion to help with that—"

"Oh, for quake's sake!" Garith burst out. "*I* made it with him!"

Ansel turned, clearly astonished.

Raffa spoke up quickly. "Garith did all the calculations."

To his dismay, Garith glowered at him. "I don't need your help. Just keep clear, why don't you?"

"Garith, please. We will discuss this at home." Ansel's voice was light, but Raffa heard a warning note in it. "Chancellor, I apologize."

The Chancellor raised her eyebrows, then inclined her head. Garith's shoulders stiffened, and he gave Raffa another scowl. It wasn't fair of Garith to be angry at him, yet Raffa felt more bewildered than resentful. He wanted to help his cousin, but he didn't know what to do—maybe because it wasn't his problem to fix.

Meanwhile, Ansel had gathered himself and was speaking again. "Well, then. The infusion . . . As I was saying . . . Raffa?"

Raffa pulled the earthenware jar from the pocket of his tunic. Kuma glared at him. In her eyes he saw the anger and hurt of betrayal, and he could tell what she was thinking: *How dare you help them dose her?*

"No," she said, her voice low and tight. "I won't need the infusion. She knows me, I can steady her without it."

"I cannot allow that," Jayney countered. "It's far too dangerous."

"I agree," Ansel said, and the Chancellor concurred, saying, "Senior Jayney is right."

They were all looking at Kuma, a solid wall of disapproval. She thrust out her chin. "No," she repeated.

Her stubbornness gave Raffa an opening. This would be his only chance. He stepped toward her and put the jar of the harmless infusion in her hand, using it as an excuse to turn them both away from the others.

"Kuma, I treated the raccoons," he said brightly. "You know that, right? I'm sure this infusion is *exactly* what Roo needs." He stared hard at her, willing her to hear what he wasn't saying: *Trust me. I have a plan.*

"Do you know, I've never actually seen a bear before?" he babbled on. "This is really exciting! Does she roar a lot? Is it very frightening?"

Kuma stared back, querying him with her eyes. She

cleared her throat. "Sometimes," she said.

"If she were to *do that now*, it might make things all *shakes and tremors*! Just give her the infusion, and get her to do what you want. And then—well, *we can all go home.*"

He forced a hearty chuckle and patted her shoulder, feeling her body tense under his hand. Did that mean she had understood?

Chancellor Leeds addressed Kuma. "We would much prefer that you be the one to give the bear the infusion, young Oriole," she said. Her voice was relaxed, but the implication was clear: If Kuma would not dose the bear, then someone else would.

Mannum Trubb cackled, and Kuma looked at the heavy spiked bluggen he was holding.

"I'll do it," she said.

Jayney walked to the shed door. He pushed it partway open. From inside, Raffa heard panting and whining sounds. Jayney reached down beside the door and brought out a bucket of water.

"The bear is caged," he said. "We have kept it thirsty so it would take the infusion."

Kuma glanced into the bucket. She emptied out half the water, then uncorked the jar and added the infusion.

"No one comes in with me," she said as she stood and picked up the bucket.

Ansel and Jayney exchanged glances. "There is a small door at the side of the cage," Jayney said. "Dose the beast first. After you show us the empty bucket, you will wait for the dose to do its work before opening the cage. I will be standing at the door."

Kuma stepped inside and closed the door behind her.

Raffa hurried to the wall of the shed and pressed his ear against it. He heard Kuma's voice murmuring indistinctly. Then the door opened, and she tossed out the bucket, empty.

Everyone waited. More murmurs from inside the shed. The muscles in Raffa's neck knotted; he bounced on his toes a little to try to relax. What was happening? Did Kuma understand what he had tried to tell her?

Then Kuma's voice came through clearly. "It's okay, Roo. It's okay— No, Roo! NO!"

She sounded on the edge of panic. Everyone outside stirred uneasily. For the first time, Jayney looked unsure of himself.

Then the door burst open. Wild-eyed and disheveled, Kuma shouted, "She's crazed—she doesn't know me! Get away! RUN!"

CHAPTER TWENTY-SIX

A mighty roar shook the shed. Another roar followed, jolting the very ground itself. The group scattered. Trubb was the first to flee; he promptly dropped the bluggen and headed for the gate, with Jayney, the Chancellor, Garith, and Ansel on his heels. Raffa ran, too, but he ducked around the corner of the shed.

Kuma was racing after the others, with Roo right behind her. "Run, everyone!" she screamed again. Then, to Raffa's amazement, she turned her head, caught his eye . . . and winked at him!

She *had* understood! Raffa knew now that she was

actually leading the bear, not being chased, and this might well give him a few more precious moments.

He dashed into the neighboring shed and slammed the door behind him. Even through the closed door, he could hear Roo's roars, as well as shouts of alarm, which were growing fainter. He scanned the space quickly. This shed was the one that housed adult animals—females, Kuma had said.

The animals were mostly awake, and calm. Raffa knew at once that they had been treated with the training infusion: Dozens of pairs of purple eyes peered at him from the cages. He was here on a hunch, and he had to hurry.

One set of shelves held raccoons. Raffa opened the hemp bag holding the twins, who immediately began to squeak.

"Mamma? Mamma?"

"Mamma! Mamma!"

On a shoulder-high shelf to his right, a raccoon frantically hurled herself against the wire door of her cage, calling out and crying in obvious desperation. The commotion woke Echo, who clicked in annoyance. Raffa took a moment to pull out the perch. The bat stretched his wings and, still upside down, squeaked in delight.

"Bando Twig mamma!" he said.

Raffa was about to open the cage when the shed door flew open. His heart bounced in his chest as he whirled around.

It was Trixin! She stumbled inside, panting. "I ran around the back first," she gasped, "but then I figured it was safer to be indoors—"

She stopped and took in the scene: Raffa's hand on the latch, the mother raccoon still frantic, the babies now crying out for her. "What are you doing?"

Raffa yanked open the cage door, grabbed the mother by the scruff, and shoved her into the hemp bag. "Trixin, listen," he said, aware of the desperation in his voice. "Kuma and I—we're leaving. There's this project—I think they might be training animals to attack people."

Trixin was gawping at him as if he had turned into a throll.

He spoke faster, his words propelled by fear. "I don't have time to explain, but what they're doing is terrible! You have to believe me! Will you help us? Tell them you saw me heading toward the Commons."

The furrow between Trixin's eyes deepened, first in doubt and confusion, and then in vexation. "I can't! If they find out I helped you, I'll lose my job, and I only just got it!"

"Please, Trixin!"

"No! You don't understand! My family—winter's coming—you can't ask me to do this!"

"Roo is Kuma's family! They hurt the twins on purpose!"

Raffa knew he was hardly making sense anymore. His brain was a complete garble.

"Kuma's with you? You're together in this?" Trixin demanded.

"Yes! She's only pretending that Roo has gone wild. It was to get everyone out of here so we could escape—"

"And you swear on—on—on your pother's oath that all this nonsense you're spouting is true?"

"I swear it's true, every word!"

Echo must have sensed his agitation, for he spread his wings, drawing Trixin's attention.

"Raffa good," Echo squeaked. "Trixin friend?"

Trixin blinked. She stared at the bat for a moment, then pressed her lips together as she looked at Raffa.

He didn't take his eyes off her as he answered Echo. "Yes, Echo. Trixin friend. I haven't known her very long, but it feels like—like longer."

Silence, except for squeaks and chitters of joy from the raccoons in the bag.

Finally Trixin heaved an enormous sigh. "Oh, all right!" she said. "But I am *not* losing my job over this. We'll have to think of something. . . ."

She glanced around, then stomped to a corner of the shed, where she picked up a stout wooden board.

"Here," she said, holding it out to him.

He looked at the board in bafflement.

"Don't you see?" she said. "You're to hit me with it—hard enough to give me a good lump. And then I can say that you knocked me out and I have no idea what you were about. Hurry and get it over with!"

Raffa stood with his mouth agape. He glanced down at the board. "I don't want to hit you—I don't think I can—"

"Quake's sake!" Trixin shouted. "Do I have to do everything myself?"

She grabbed the board with both hands, swung it hard, and bashed it into her forehead.

"YOW!" she shrieked, and staggered as she dropped the board.

Raffa grabbed her arm and helped her sit down against the wall. Already a handsome lump was swelling above her eyebrow.

"Now get out of here," she said, rubbing the lump. "This is going to hurt for days, and I don't want it to be for nothing!"

He grabbed the raccoons' bag and ran.

It was not easy to run while holding on to a bag in which an ecstatic raccoon reunion was taking place. Raffa raced out of the shed toward the gate, but he was hampered by the awkwardness of the bag and the weight of the mother. He hadn't had time to put Echo back on the perch; the bat clung to his sleeve.

At the gate he pulled up and looked around in a panic. He saw that the fleeing group had been joined by the gate guard and the wagon driver. Kuma and Roo had chased them down the drive toward the stable yard. He heard Ansel shout, "Garith! To the laboratory! Hurry!"

Raffa turned and dashed down the length of the fence, then into the brush, where he had hidden the night before. "Echo," he panted, "go toward the stables. Find Kuma and Roo and lead them to me. I'm going to go on, to the west. Toward sunfall, okay?"

"Echo go, Kuma come," the bat said, and flapped off.

Raffa hated seeing Echo fly out of sight, but he could think of no other way to reunite with Kuma. He hoisted the raccoons' bag over his shoulder and started off to the west.

In the opposite direction, to the east of Gilden, lay the ferry landing, the river, home. But he knew it was the first place they would search. He planned to head west, into the foothills, and camp there for a while. Maybe he could somehow circle south of Gilden and find another way to cross the Everwide.

Sooner than he dared hope, Echo was back. "Kuma come," he said. "Big big big BIG—"

"That's Roo, Echo," Raffa said. "She's a bear."

"Stop," Echo said. "Raffa run no good."

What was Echo saying? That he should turn back?

"I shouldn't run, Echo? What do you mean?"

"Raffa run, big bear run."

He understood then: Kuma had told Echo to convey that Raffa shouldn't be running when they reunited; if he did, Roo would chase him.

It worked out well, considering that Raffa had to stand still and watch as the giant bear loped toward him. Roo looked far bigger than when he had seen her emerging from the shed.

Kuma was running alongside the bear. She slowed to a walk as Roo raised her nose in the air. "Stay here,

Roo," she said. Then she hurried the rest of the way to Raffa and, to his surprise, gave him a hug.

"See, Roo?" She turned to look at the bear while her arms were still around Raffa's shoulders. "Raffa is my friend. Come meet him."

So the hug had been for Roo's benefit. But Raffa didn't care; he was so relieved to see Kuma again that he hugged her back.

As the bear ambled over, Kuma cautioned Raffa. "Don't move. Let her smell you. I know we're in a rush, but she has to do this."

Raffa did as he was told. Roo made a thorough job of it, including an extended bout of sniffing with her snout between his legs. Raffa squeaked in alarm, which made Kuma giggle.

"Most animals do that, smell each other's—um, lower parts," she said.

"Of course," Raffa said, trying not to flinch from Roo's probing nose.

Apparently satisfied, Roo turned her attention to Raffa's rucksack. Hastily he took out an apple. He held it out cautiously, and Roo swiped it from him with a snort of approval.

"Now you're friends for life," Kuma said, smiling.

But her smile vanished quickly. "Listen, we chased them toward the stables. We stopped when Echo came. The Chancellor saw us turn off the track, and started screaming for the guards. And she kept yelling about the bear—that they had to get the bear." She swallowed. "We need to take Roo somewhere safe. Where they'll never find her."

"This way," Raffa said. As they started toward the foothills, he explained his reasoning as to why they shouldn't run east. Echo flew ahead of them, sometimes circling back to squeak encouragement. The foothills would have forest growth for cover. If they could just make it there, they might have a chance to elude pursuit.

They came to a low stone wall topped by a hedgerow. Roo broke through the thorny hedge as if it were made of matchsticks. On the other side lay a straw-stubbled field. For a brief, long moment, Raffa stared through the gap at the field.

Wide open.

No cover anywhere.

"Come on," Kuma said. "At least we'll be able to move fast."

The field looked enormous. Raffa felt almost naked with all that open space around him, and nothing but a menacing gray sky above.

Roo covered the ground easily, and Kuma ran light-footed as a doe. But Raffa found that the furrows were exactly the wrong distance apart—too far for a single stride, too close together for two. If he were to twist an ankle, he'd have to ignore the pain and keep going.

Echo flew back toward the hedgerow to scout behind the group, then veered sharply and returned. He hovered over Raffa and squeaked; still running, Raffa held up his arm so the bat could land.

"Ouch!" Echo flapped in agitation. "Birds! Many!"

Raffa looked over his shoulder and almost tripped. Catching his balance and his breath, he searched the sky behind them, seeing nothing but clouds.

"What kind of birds, Echo?" he asked urgently.

"Craw, craw," Echo replied.

Crows. Raffa frowned in puzzlement. What were the crows going to do—drop pastries on them?

"Raffa!" Kuma was pointing not to the sky overhead but much lower, on a line with the horizon. A dark cluster was moving steadily toward them.

"They've probably been sent to track us," she said. "We should split up. Once we get to the hills, you can send Echo to find me again."

Raffa didn't answer. Something was bothering him . . . something that kept ducking away from the grasp of his mind. Crows at the Chancellor's dinner . . . No, that wasn't it—

"We can't just stand here!" Kuma said in a near-wail. Roo whined, sensing Kuma's distress.

Whatever the memory was, it wouldn't come to him. "Let's stay together until we get across the field," Raffa said, "and split up once we hit the scrub."

They would never be able to traverse the field before the crows reached them, but they ran anyway. When they were no more than a third of the way across, the first of the crows swooped above them.

What came next happened so quickly that Raffa could hardly believe it had happened at all. The crow let out a loud *craw* and dove directly at his head.

"Yow!" he cried.

The bird had struck hard with its beak. Then the rest of the crows were upon them.

One after another, the crows dove and struck, always aiming for their heads, sometimes landing a vicious peck on their shoulders. There were perhaps two dozen of them, but to Raffa it seemed like hundreds.

Echo was squealing and flapping, trying to impede

the crows despite being barely a quarter their size.

"No, Echo, don't!" Raffa yelled, terrified that the bat would get hurt. "Stay out of the way!"

Kuma screamed as one crow struck her dangerously near her left eye. Blood bloomed on her brow, and the image that had been eluding Raffa solidified in his mind.

The scarecrows, their blank eyes gaping.

The ground around the scarecrows littered with crushed grapes.

"Eyes!" he shrieked. "They're going for our eyes!"

CHAPTER TWENTY-SEVEN

RAFFA threw himself to the ground and buried his face in the crook of his elbow. The sack holding the raccoons went flying. He heard Kuma's desperate voice saying, "Down, Roo! Down! Raffa, help! I can't get her down!"

A crow struck at Raffa's neck, piercing the flesh behind his ear. He bellowed a curse, then raised his head and saw Kuma frantically beating off crows with one arm while hanging on to Roo with the other.

Raffa jumped to his feet. His arm over his brow, he rushed toward Kuma and the bear. There were crows all around her, flapping, cawing, striking. . . .

"Kuma! Get down, protect yourself!"

"No! I can't let them blind Roo!"

"But they're not attacking her, only us! Get down, I'm telling you—!"

Raffa did the only thing he could think of: He threw himself at Kuma and grabbed her around the waist, taking her down with a hard tackle. She cried out and struggled against him as the crows continued to dive at them, raining blows on their heads and shoulders.

With his body holding Kuma down, Raffa yelled into her ear. "Cover your eyes! Trust me!"

She stopped fighting him and obeyed. He let her roll over, and she peeked out from under her arm. Her eyes widened: She'd seen that he was telling the truth.

Then Roo gave a tremendous roar right over Raffa's head. With his back to the bear, he couldn't see what she was doing, but then there was a thudding sound, followed by an explosion of black feathers.

The bear roared again, and Raffa turned to see Roo swatting at the crows with her enormous paws. The birds were clustered so thickly that every blow clouted away at least one crow, sometimes two.

Still, the others continued to attack. Then Raffa shouted to Kuma, "Make yourself smaller!" They crouched as close together as they could, arms crossed over their heads, giving the crows the tightest possible target.

With another roar, Roo cleared several birds in a single swipe. That was enough for the rest of them: In a final flurry of angry croaks, the remaining crows flapped into the air and flew off toward the Commons.

A weighty silence followed the crows' departure. As Raffa finally, hesitantly, lowered his arms, he heard Kuma's gasps for breath alternating with his own.

From a few paces away came the feeble croak of a crow as it died.

There were eleven dead crows on the ground. Raffa and Kuma knelt over one of them, its neck twisted at an odd angle. Raffa felt compelled to straighten it gently, so it looked more comfortable in death.

"It wasn't their fault," Kuma whispered.

Roo snuffled at her, whining a little.

"Or yours, either," she added sadly, fondling the bear's ears.

Raffa was still trying to understand what had just happened. Training crows to blind people! As a wartime tactic, it was one thing, but he shuddered to think of the callousness of someone trying to blind him and Kuma, who could hardly be called an enemy army.

He doubted that Mannum Trubb had the authority to order such an attack. It might have been Jayney. Or even Chancellor Leeds herself. And each of those possibilities served to block the one he didn't want to consider: That it was Uncle Ansel who had done it.

Raffa glared at his own thoughts and forced his mind back to the present. "We have to go," he said. He adjusted the straps of his rucksack. Then, in a moment of sudden realization, he looked around wildly.

"The babies!" he cried out. "Where are they?"

The hemp bag was on the ground several paces away; it looked suspiciously flat and inert. Was it empty?

Raffa raced over, groped for the top of the bag and opened it. The face of a dazed-looking baby raccoon peered out at him. He couldn't tell which one it was.

"Mamma? Bando? Bando? Mamma?"

It was Twig, and she was alone.

Raffa cried out in distress. "We have to find them!" He cradled Twig as he scanned the field. It was all his fault. He didn't even remember dropping the sack when the crows had begun their attack.

The mother raccoon sensing danger. Picking up Bando

in her mouth, finding her way out of the sack, and carrying her baby—where?—to a place safer than the open field. "She'll come back for Twig, I know she will!"

Kuma looked as miserable as he felt. "We have to go, Raffa," she said gently. "She wouldn't have turned back, so she must be somewhere up ahead. Maybe we'll find her. Or she'll find us, so long as we keep Twig with us."

Raffa knew she was right. The crows had been only the first wave, he was sure upon certain. They had to get away before . . . before whatever came next.

He put Twig back into the bag. They began tramping over the furrows again. Raffa tried to hurry, but his legs felt as stiff and heavy as tree trunks. At each step he scanned the field, hoping to spot the missing raccoons.

The only small comfort was that Twig seemed stronger now, having had the chance to nurse from her mother. A quiet but steady stream of plaintive *Mamma*s and *Bando*s issued from the bag. Raffa could hardly bear it: Just when the baby raccoon had been reunited with her mother, they were separated again, and this time, there was no Bando for solace.

When they finally reached the end of the field, Raffa sent Echo back to scout. The rest of them ducked into the scrub and sheltered under a small hazeltine tree.

They drank from Raffa's waterskin. Then Raffa hastily cleaned up the wound on Kuma's forehead, and did the same with his own neck. He knew he couldn't take the time to make a poultice, but he rolled a few yellowroot leaves between his palms and plastered the leaves to their injuries.

"Why didn't the crows attack Roo?" Kuma asked.

"Because she's too valuable to them," Raffa said. "I'm almost certain they want to use her as a weapon—I'll explain more later. She'd be no good to them blind."

Kuma looked stricken, which made Raffa wonder if his words had been too stark. But there was no time for honey-dripping. They had to face things as they were.

Just then Echo returned and alit on a branch over Raffa's head.

"Many," the bat said.

"What, Echo? Many what?"

"Man horse."

The guards were coming, and they were coming on horseback.

"Stop," Echo said. "Stop stop stop!"

Raffa froze and looked around, eyes wide and nerves jangling. "What is it?" he whispered.

"Go," Echo said.

"Echo, which is it—stop or go?" Raffa didn't mean to sound cross, but his anxiety was making him impatient.

"Man horse stop."

"One of the guards has stopped?"

"Many stop. Many many."

"They've all stopped?" Raffa couldn't understand it. Why would the guards have stopped pursuing them? "Where? At the field?"

"Stop wait field."

From where he was sitting, Raffa could see only the nearest part of the field. The guards must be on the far side. He tried to think. They were waiting for something. Reinforcements, maybe?

No matter: He and Kuma had to take advantage of it. He jumped to his feet. "Come on," he said to Kuma. "Echo, would you fly over the field and tell me when they've started moving again?"

Echo rose into the air. Raffa had taken only a few steps out from under the tree when he heard a high-pitched squeal. He looked up and saw Echo diving, so fast that he was only a blur. The bat dropped out of the sky onto his arm.

"Bird! Hurt claw!" the bat shrieked. He tried to

burrow under Raffa's tunic, shrieking, squealing, wings thrashing and claws scrabbling.

Raffa's heart was hammering; the bat's panic was contagious. He reached for Echo gingerly, afraid of hurting the tiny creature. "It's okay, Echo, shussss—"

Somehow he got hold of the frantic bat and held him gently but firmly. Then he put Echo on his perch and tucked the necklace under his tunic. He pulled at the neckline so he could look down at Echo. "You're safe now. Can you talk?"

"Bird—hurt—claw," Echo said, still panting.

A raptor. Could it be the same one that had attacked the twins? "The babies, Echo? The bird that hurt Bando and Twig?"

But Echo hadn't seen the attack on the twins. So how would he know—

"Bird hurt *Echo*!" the bat cried in anguish.

Raffa gasped. No wonder Echo was so terrified! He looked up and began searching the sky wildly.

Then he heard a high, thin, whining sound. He had never heard a sound quite like it before, and it made him uneasy.

The sound grew louder. It seemed to be coming from somewhere up above. Raffa frowned: His head had begun to ache a little.

In the sky above the field, he saw a single bird on the wing: an enormous owl. It was headed directly toward him.

And it was screaming.

CHAPTER TWENTY-EIGHT

THE owl's screams were like knives of sound. Raffa's teeth were rattling. His legs seemed to have turned to porridge. With his whole body quivering, he raised his hands to put his fingers in his ears, but his hands were shaking so hard he could barely control them. Even though Garith had told him about this sound, Raffa could never have imagined anything so horrible.

As he sank to his knees, he realized that this was why Ansel and Garith had rushed off to the laboratory: to get the infusion that had made the squirrel scream. And to feed it to the owl, which was now in the midst of accomplishing its mission of screaming Raffa into unconsciousness. The pain of his uncle's betrayal was as sharp as the agony in his ears.

In that moment, he also knew why the mounted guards had stopped. They were keeping themselves out of hearing range of the owl.

Involuntary tears rolled hot and fast down his cheeks. On the perch necklace, Echo had gone utterly still, and Raffa knew that the little bat had already lost consciousness. The same fate, he was sure, had befallen Twig.

Raffa saw Kuma's knees buckle. She slumped to the ground, her hands uselessly over her ears, her face contorted in pain. Roo was twisting her head and neck; her mouth was wide open in a roar, but Raffa heard only the owl's screams.

The owl flew in circles overhead. It must have had to draw breath, but to Raffa, its screams had merged into a single endless shriek. Through the blur of tears, he saw dots swimming in front of his eyes. He blinked hard several times. The dots vanished . . . except for one.

Raffa fought to stay upright and saw that the dot was clearly a person—someone running toward him across the field. Whoever it was, they would soon be within range of the owl's monstrous powers.

But the person continued to race forward at top speed. Though his thoughts were by now little more than scraps and shreds, Raffa managed to wonder why the runner was unaffected by the owl's screams.

The figure drew nearer. With a shock, Raffa recognized the way the person was running: He'd seen that gait hundreds of times, maybe thousands.

Garith.

The owl's shrieks stabbed into the core of Raffa's brain. He fell forward onto his hands and knees, struggling to keep his head up and his eyes on Garith.

Garith stopped running. His arm began to whirl—was it whirling? Or was Raffa seeing things, his vision a blur, his awareness lacerated by the horrendous noise? No, Garith's arm was definitely in motion. . . .

Then something flew out of his hand—something with a long tail. Raffa saw it for only the merest moment before it soared from sight.

His strength finally left him. He slumped onto his face as the world blurred into blackness.

"Raffa, wake up! We have to hurry! Please!"

Raffa opened his eyes and saw a face. It was Garith. But it didn't sound like Garith. His voice sounded . . .

strange somehow. Oddly flat.

"Come on now," Garith said. "A few deep breaths." He helped Raffa to his feet. Raffa swayed dizzily and leaned on Garith's arm.

His vision cleared and his eyes widened at what he saw: Several paces away, a great-tufted owl lay on the ground. Raffa was all but certain it was the same one that had chased him and Garith in the Forest. One wing was bent under it; the other, only partly outstretched, was longer than his arm.

Roo pushed herself to all fours, groaning. She shook like a dog from head to tail for several seconds, then nosed Kuma and whined piteously.

Raffa limped to where Kuma lay. As he bent over her, she opened her eyes. "Is Roo all right?" were her first words. She sat up slowly, and Roo bellowed in delight.

The ground beneath Raffa's feet began to rumble from the pounding hoofbeats of dozens of horses.

"We have to go!" Garith said in his strange flat voice. With Kuma and Raffa still dazed, they started jogging toward the foothills.

"Hills up ahead . . . trees," Garith panted. Raffa knew what he meant. The horses would have to slow down on a forested hillside. As long as Raffa's group stayed off the trails, they should be able to avoid the guards and find a place to hide.

They spoke no more, needing every breath for running.

A squeak sounded from under Raffa's tunic: Echo was awake now, too. Raffa slowed enough to take out the perch. The bat was grooming himself furiously, as if to wipe away any remains of the owl's screams.

Dusk was giving way to dark; Echo became their eyes. He kept track of where the guards were, directing Raffa's group on a zigzag course away from their pursuers. They waded into a stream and followed it uphill to confuse any hunt hounds the guards might be using. Raffa held the hemp bag above his head to keep Twig from getting wet.

Dripping and chilled through, they crested the hill and scrambled down the other side. Near the bottom, Echo found a cluster of boulders that formed a hollow. It wasn't big enough to be a cave, but it provided some shelter.

They couldn't risk lighting a fire, for fear that the guards would see the smoke, so they huddled around Roo as close as they dared. Raffa was grateful for the warmth, even if it did smell powerfully of bear. He checked on Twig, who seemed confused and sad but otherwise unharmed.

Echo flew off and returned to report that the guards had already turned back. It was a relief, but a short-lived one.

"We can't stay here long," Raffa said. "As soon as it's light, they'll send birds to track us. We have to get as far as we can tonight."

There was no response from Garith, who was staring at the ground.

"Garith."

No response again.

The suspicion that had been nudging at Raffa now ballooned into dread.

"Garith," he repeated, and this time he put a hand on his cousin's knee.

Scowling, Garith shook off Raffa's hand. He raised his head, and Raffa saw fear and uncertainty in his cousin's eyes.

Raffa swallowed hard. He knew now what had happened. It was more than a guess: He could see it all clearly in his mind.

Garith had gone to the laboratory with Ansel, to fetch the infusion that would make the owl scream.

Without his father's knowledge, Garith had used another infusion—the one Raffa had created but not given to the crow.

Garith had dosed *himself* . . . with the infusion made to cause deafness.

He had done it so he could get close to the owl. The thing he had thrown was a stone on a cord, and he had brought down the owl with it.

Raffa stared at Garith. "You—you—" He could not find the words.

"I had to do it," Garith said, his voice too loud. "You wouldn't have gotten away otherwise."

Raffa still couldn't speak. It was as if the thought was too enormous to fit into his brain at one time. The infusion had been totally untested; its effects might well be permanent. Garith . . . deaf . . . because of him . . .

"Raffa, I swear I didn't know," Garith went on. "About—well, practically everything, it turns out. Da told me—just like he said to you. Training animals to do human stuff. He only told me just now about using them to fight, and that's why they have to have the bear."

He guffawed, but it was a grim sound. "I was only ever allowed in the first shed, the empty one. I saw the scarecrows once and asked about them. Trubb said it was so the birds could get used to being around a lot of people. I believed him—how stupid can a person be? Senior Jayney trained those crows. He's the one who sent them after you."

His eyes filled with tears, and he dropped his head again. "But it was Da who sent the owl," he said.

Raffa's throat swelled. It was bad enough, Ansel being his uncle. He couldn't imagine what it must feel like for Garith.

A heavy silence filled the little space. With a thud in his gut, Raffa realized that silence was the only thing Garith could hear now.

Echo fluttered to Garith's arm. Garith looked up in surprise. He held out a finger, and Echo moved to perch there, upside down as usual.

"Raffa friend no good?" the bat asked.

Raffa cleared his throat. "Echo, this is Garith," he said softly. "You met him once before, but I don't think I ever had the chance to introduce you. And, yes, he's our friend."

Friend. Cousin. The closest thing to a brother Raffa would ever have.

"Echo, Garith is the one who—who stopped the owl."

"Garith good!" Echo squeaked excitedly, and Raffa nodded in agreement.

Garith snorted. "You look like you think—like he's talking to you, or something."

Now it was Raffa's turn to be surprised. He had forgotten that Garith didn't yet know about Echo's ability to speak.

Raffa pointed at Echo, then tapped his fingers against his thumb like a mouth talking. "The scarlet vine," he added, and made a snakelike motion with his hand.

As Garith stared at the bat, Raffa watched his cousin's expression change from skepticism to uncertainty, and then to wonder.

Echo looked right at Garith and said, "Garith BIG good."

Raffa repeated the words with a gesture. Garith coughed out a laugh of amazement. "Shakes and tremors," he mumbled. He stroked Echo gently before returning him to the perch.

Then he grinned at Raffa. "I got the owl on my first try," he said. "And not a word from you about it being luck. That was better than good—it was pure brilliant skill."

His words were still too loud, his laugh a coarse bray.

It made Raffa flinch inwardly, but at the same time he had to smile. Garith was still Garith.

Raffa wondered if he would have done the same in his cousin's place. Within his own thoughts, he forced himself to be honest: He wouldn't have been brave enough. Garith had not only taken a dire physical risk, he had defied his father, utterly.

Then and there, Raffa made a silent vow to find an antidote that would restore Garith's hearing. He knew now that experimenting would take its own kind of bravery, most of all the willingness to fail. As far as he knew, deafness had never been cured by an infusion.

But just because it *hadn't* been done didn't mean it *couldn't* be done. He'd start with the scarlet vine. If that didn't work, he'd try every combination he could think of. No matter how long it took, he would never give up.

His eyes met Garith's. "It was better than brilliant," Raffa said.

Garith nodded proudly even though he hadn't heard. And Raffa remembered all the times they had understood each other without words.

Raffa held out his hands, palms flat and together, so Garith could clap them. Then Kuma joined in with another clap so all their hands were joined . . . Raffa's, surrounded by those of his friends.

The celebration lasted exactly the length of those two claps, for the problems they now faced were too numerous to count. In Raffa's mind, they heaped themselves one upon another until the whole pile collapsed into a chaos of thought.

A battle seemed imminent—one that was an utter mystery. The Chancellor appeared determined to recapture Roo. Hundreds of other animals were still trapped in the sheds.

Bando and the mother raccoon were missing. Raffa's parents would arrive in Gilden and learn that he was gone; Raffa felt sore all over at the thought of their worry. He and his friends needed food and rest, but they also had to get as far away from Gilden as they could—with luck, to a place where Roo would forever be out of human reach.

The perch around Raffa's neck swayed a little. Echo looked up at him with those enormous eyes . . . eyes that should have been black, not purple.

Raffa bowed his head and cupped his hand around the little bat. "Echo good," he whispered.

Echo blinked. "Need skeeto," he whispered back.

Raffa couldn't help a grin, and felt his spirits lift a little.

Get to the mountains. That was the first thing. Hiding in the mountains would give them what they most needed: time to figure out everything else.

He heaved himself upright, reluctantly leaving the warmth exuded by Roo. "Time to go," he said. A thud to his gut again: Garith couldn't hear him.

But Garith had seen him stand and was already on his feet. With Kuma between them, they stepped out of the hollow together.

The Sudden Mountains lay ahead of them, their peaks a jagged threat against the murky sky. In the deepest part of the night, with the bat as their guide, the two boys and the girl, and the bear and the baby raccoon, began walking toward the west, where none of them had ever been before.

ACKNOWLEDGMENTS

Sincere thanks to . . .

Abby Ranger, who edited this story with endless patience and astute guidance.

Joe Merkel for the book's beautiful design.

Jim Madsen for the perfect cover art and interior illustrations.

Mark Schley for the wonderful map (say it with me: "I just LOVE maps in fantasy novels!").

Jim Armstrong for all the little things.

The *Wing & Claw* team at HarperCollins, including Kate Morgan Jackson, Lindsey Karl, Alejandra Oliva, Tiffany Liao, Bethany Reis, Patty Rosati, and Matt Schweitzer.

The HC sales reps, without whom this book would be forever unread.

Ginger Knowlton for being awesome, and everyone at Curtis Brown Ltd.

Julie Damerell for assistance above and beyond the call.

The Society of Children's Book Writers and Illustrators, the Rochester Area Children's Writers and Illustrators, and We Need Diverse Books, for their support and encouragement.

The many schools, students, teachers, and librarians who have hosted and inspired me over the years.

Brighton Memorial Library, where I wrote most of this book.

Friends: M. T. Anderson, Julia Durango, Marsha Hayles, Theresa Nelson, Margo Rabb, Vivian Vande-Velde, and the Lunch Bunch, for breaking bread with me, making me laugh, and listening to me whine.

My family, especially Anna, Sean, Margaret, Craig, and Ed.

And most of all, my love and thanks to Ben and Callan, who waved good-bye cheerfully whenever I left to write, and never failed to welcome me home.

CAVERN OF SECRETS

CHAPTER ONE

THE wind stirred the green needles of the never-bare trees. They swayed and leaned toward each other, murmuring of the coming spring.

The trees surrounded the entrance to a cave, which was partially blocked by a huge lichen-covered boulder. Or perhaps it was a pile of dried bracken, for it, too, trembled in the wind.

Then the pile began to stretch and shift, taking on a more distinct shape. A shaggy head . . . an enormous torso . . .

The gigantic golden bear seemed to be emerging from the mountain itself. She opened her mouth and growled, a low rumble that grew into a throaty roar.

* * *

Raffa was woken by thunder.

Odd upon strange, he thought. *A thunderstorm at this time of year?* He rubbed his eyes and saw Kuma sitting up on her pallet.

"That's her—she's awake!" Kuma exclaimed in delight, and jumped to her feet.

As Raffa followed her out of the shelter, he marveled at the thought of a bear so big that he'd mistaken her growl for thunder.

They stopped just short of the mouth of the cave. The bear stood on her hind legs, half again as tall as a man, and sniffed the air for several seconds. Back down on all fours, she shook herself so hard that fur flew like snow.

Raffa could see joy and relief on Kuma's face. It was one thing to know that bears hibernate. It was quite another for Kuma to have seen her beloved Roo breathing so infrequently for so many weeks, almost as if she had forgotten how.

Moments of joy had been all but absent for Raffa's little group that winter. There in the desolate wilderness of the Sudden Mountains, they were forced to spend their hours focused entirely on two activities: keeping warm and finding food. The work was too hard, the wind too cold, the snow too deep. There was never enough to eat.

Two days ago, the wind had changed. Its knife-edged sharpness had dulled, then softened. Never in his life had Raffa felt such relief over a shift in the weather. Since then, Kuma had been checking the cave obsessively to see if Roo was awake.

Now Raffa hung back while Kuma entered the cave. She moved slowly and spoke in a soothing tone as she approached the bear. Squatting down in front of Roo, she made herself small and unthreatening, and let Roo sniff at her.

Roo whined and swatted Kuma's shoulder affectionately with an enormous paw. Kuma was ready for this and had braced herself; otherwise, Roo's exuberant greeting might have knocked her over. Then the bear turned away and began nosing at something on the ground.

Something gray and furry, with a striped tail.

The mound of fur did not respond at first, but Roo let out a plaintive growl and persisted, continuing to nudge with her nose.

Finally, there was a mew of protest, and the masked face of a young raccoon appeared. Twig unfurled herself, sat up, and blinked a few times, her eyes glowing purple.

"Water?" she squeaked.

Raffa smiled at Twig and went to fetch a strawful of melted snow. He gave her a drink. When she was finished, she pawed at the bear's leg. Roo seemed fully awake and reoriented now. She relaxed, sat down, and allowed Kuma to give her a good hard scratch. At the same time, she began giving Twig a tongue-bath.

The girl scratching the bear grooming the raccoon . . . Seeing the three of them together, Raffa felt a sharp pang of longing for his own special companion.

He made his way to the back corner of the cave. A tiny bat hung there, on a perch made out of a twig tied to a leather cord. Raffa blew on the bat's whiskers. Echo stirred, then produced an annoyed click.

Delighted, Raffa tried again, blowing a little harder.

Another click, this one weaker than the first.

Raffa frowned. Neither Twig nor Echo were true hibernators like Roo, but both had slept for days at a time throughout the winter. Raffa didn't know if it was normal for bats to emerge from torpor later than raccoons. He donned the perch necklace; perhaps the warmth of his body would help Echo waken.

Echo hadn't spoken for weeks. How Raffa missed their conversations! The bat never failed to make him laugh. He could hardly wait for Echo to talk again, for then it would truly be spring, a farewell forever to this harsh winter of too little laughter.

Garith was sitting partway up inside the shelter. He had been woken not by the bear's growls but by a shaft of sunlight piercing the screen of branches.

"Garith." Raffa waved his hand to get his cousin's attention. "Roo and Twig are awake. Want to go see them?" He spoke slowly, enunciating each syllable as clearly as he could and making exaggerated gestures.

"I've told you a million times, that doesn't help me!" Garith said. "Stop talking to me like I'm some kind of idiot. I lost my *hearing*, not my brain."

His voice had flattened out since he had become deaf, and was often toneless. Raffa should have been used to it by now, but every reminder of Garith's deafness twisted his insides—because it was his fault. Maybe not directly, but the fact remained that Garith wouldn't be deaf if it weren't for Raffa's decision to flee Gilden.

Raffa had spent the winter months trying to make it up to Garith, by helping with his share of the work. But Garith resented that too, and Raffa felt as if he was always tiptoeing around his cousin's bad moods.

He didn't know what to do about it. For the hundredth time, he wished he could talk to his parents.

But he couldn't risk going home, for none of them had any idea what awaited them there. Were their families being watched? Would neighbors turn them in? Would guards seize them the instant they were sighted?

Raffa and Kuma and Garith could hardly be considered enemies of Obsidia. But Chancellor Leeds viewed them as a threat, for she knew that they possessed something more important than strength or power.

Knowledge.

Now that Raffa knew about the animals trapped in a compound, where they were being dosed and trained against their natures, he was sure that the Chancellor was seeking a way to silence him. He had nightmare visions of being thrown into the underground cells of the Garrison, left to a life not worth living among the rats and the filth and the loneliness.

And the Chancellor wanted one thing even more than his silence: Roo. Raffa had heard only dark and murky whispers of her plans, but he did know that she wanted to use the great bear as a weapon. Keeping Roo out of her reach was the main reason he and his friends had chosen to hide in the Suddens.

Now that spring had finally arrived, he found himself in an agony of indecision.

They couldn't stay here forever, but they couldn't go home, either.

Raffa slept poorly that night, waking several times to check on Echo. The next morning, the bat seemed even more inert. Raffa could see that Echo was still breathing, but his tiny body was barely warm to the touch.

He showed the bat to Kuma. "I don't know what's wrong," he said. "He should at least be starting to wake by now."

Kuma examined Echo. "Yes, I think so, too," she said slowly. "I'm sure that I've seen bats flying around in early spring."

Raffa's alarm was growing by the moment. He scolded himself silently: Panicking would do Echo no good. He thought of his parents, Mohan and Salima. When they were treating patients, they were almost always calm and deliberate. Sometimes decisions had to be made quickly. Sometimes their actions were urgent. But they were never panicky.

Think like they would. Like an apothecary.

Because Raffa did not know exactly what was wrong

with Echo, any treatment he used would have to be mild—one sure to do no harm.

A restorative tonic, then. He had only a few botanical supplies with him, and no equipment other than his trusty mortar and pestle. He set about grinding some anjella root, then combined it with dried mellia and wortjon.

Three times a day for the next two days, Raffa dosed the bat with the combination. He checked on him constantly, even massaging Echo's tiny back in an attempt to improve his circulation.

All to no avail. If anything, the bat was worse off, for no matter how many times Raffa blew on his whiskers, Echo did not respond.

Raffa made the same infusion again, but this time he added a powder made of the stems and leaves of the scarlet vine. He had taken the entire stock of the vine from Uncle Ansel's glasshouse in Gilden, and had dried the plants to store them.

Unlike the fresh vine, the dry powder emitted not a single spark or gleam when combined with other ingredients. Raffa concentrated hard while making the infusion. Nothing came to him—no moment of color or music, no prick of discomfort. No sign at all from his intuition, which was his special gift as an apothecary.

What was he to think of this blankness? Was it possible that he was losing his gift? It made him feel frightened and uncertain to have to rely solely on his training and experience instead. Did other apothecaries have to do that all the time?

He took a deep breath, gritted his teeth, and dosed Echo with the infusion.

The next few hours dragged by so slowly that it felt to Raffa as if the sun had come to a complete standstill. He looked down the neck of his tunic every few moments, hoping to detect even the smallest change in Echo's condition.

Nothing.

The bat remained as he was, limp except for the tiny claws closed tightly around the twig.

Raffa's relief that the infusion seemed to have done no harm was overwhelmed by the harsh disappointment that it had done no good, either. He went to Kuma and Garith, fighting back tears.

"I don't know what else to do," he said. "He should be awake by now, but nothing's working."

Garith glanced at Echo hanging limply from his perch. Then he looked at Raffa. "You need more botanicals," he said in a monotone. "It's still too cold up here—nothing's growing."

"And maybe . . ." Kuma's voice was soft with sympathy. "Maybe you could use some help—somebody to talk to about what you could try."

Raffa swallowed past the lump in his throat and put his hand protectively over the wee bat. Months earlier, he had saved Echo's life. Somehow that gave him a solemn responsibility for the bat. He hadn't failed Echo the first time. He couldn't fail him now.

He clenched and unclenched his jaw. Garith and Kuma were both right, and he was sure upon certain about what he had to do. When he spoke, the words came out fiercely.

"We're going home," he said.

Neither Garith nor Kuma uttered a single protest. They were well aware of the risks; at the same time, Raffa knew that each had reasons for wanting to leave the Suddens. Kuma needed to find a safe place for Roo, somewhere close enough to visit occasionally. And Garith had to go back to face his father, a meeting that Raffa suspected was both yearned for and dreaded.

"All right, then," Raffa said. "We'll leave tomorrow at daybirth."

He glanced down at Echo on the perch around his neck. "I'll get there as fast as I can, I promise," he murmured.

Ford the Everwide . . . Find a hideout for Roo . . . And then go home, where—as long as no guards awaited him—there would be plenty of botanicals to work with.

Even more important, his parents would be there. Mohan, with his profound knowledge of garden botanicals, and Salima, so familiar with wild plants; both of them having years of experience treating illness and injury. Surely, with their help, he could cure the little bat.

Then Raffa's stomach lurched at his next thought.

If only Echo lives long enough to get there.

FROM NEWBERY MEDAL–WINNING AUTHOR
LINDA SUE PARK
COMES A NEW MAGICAL TRILOGY

WING & CLAW

Raffa Santana's journey continues
into the wilderness of the Sudden Peaks
and beyond. There, botanical discoveries,
help from new and old friends, and his own
courage will determine the future of the
Forest of Wonders and the fate of the
people of all of Obsidia.

HARPER
An Imprint of HarperCollinsPublishers
www.harpercollinschildrens.com